The Resistible Rise of Arturo Ui

A Gangster Spectacle

by Bertolt Brecht

Adapted by George Tabori

Music by Hans-Dieter Hosalla

SAMUEL FRENCH

FOUNDED 1830

New York Hollywood London Toronto

SAMUELFRENCH.COM

MUSIC

Music for this production is available on a rental and deposit basis.

Royalty for use of the music is $10.00 for each performance. We can lend you a piano score of the music, for a period of eight weeks, on receipt of the following:

1. Number of performances and exact performance dates.

2. Royalty in full on the music for the entire production.

3. Deposit of $10.00, which is refunded on return of the material in good condition immediately after your production. Plus first-class postage and handling charge of 75¢ for the piano score.

*The following credits are from the program of the New York
production which premiered Nov. 11, 1963*

LUNT-FONTANNE
THEATRE

DAVID MERRICK

presents

CHRISTOPHER PLUMMER

in

BERTOLT BRECHT'S
ARTURO UI

Adapted by
GEORGE TABORI

Directed by
TONY RICHARDSON

Designed by
ROUBEN TER-ARUTUNIAN

Associate Producer NEIL HARTLEY

with

ELISHA COOK	MICHAEL CONSTANTINE	LIONEL STANDER
HUGH FRANKLIN	HENRY LASCOE	ROGER DE KOVEN
	MURVYN VYE	

Leonardo Cimino   James Coco   James Frawley   Harold Gary
Louis Guss Dossie Hollingsworth Paul Michael Tom Pedi
Beah Richards   Warren Wade   Robert Weil

and

MADELEINE SHERWOOD

5

CHARACTERS

THE BARKER

FLAKE

CARUTHER

BUTCHER   *Businessmen, leaders of the Cauliflower Trust*

MULBERRY

CLARK

SHEET, *a shipping tycoon*

OLD DOGSBOROUGH

YOUNG DOGSBOROUGH

ARTURO UI, *gangster boss*

ERNESTO ROMA, *his sidekick*

TED RAGG, *reporter on* The Star

DOCKDAISY, *a moll*

EMANUELE GIRI, *gangster*

BOWL, *Sheet's treasurer*

GOODWILL and GAFFLES, *gentlemen from City Hall*

O'CASEY, *chairman of the investigating committee*

THE ACTOR

GIUSEPPE ("THE FLORIST") GIVOLA, *gangster*

CROCKET, *wholesale vegetable merchant*

A LITTLE GIRL

GREENWOOL, *a baritone*

6

THE DEFENDANT FISH

THE DEFENSE COUNSEL

THE JUDGE

THE COURT PHYSICIAN

THE PROSECUTOR

A WOUNDED WOMAN

YOUNG INNA, *Roma's boyfriend*

SHORTY

IGNATIUS DULLFEET, *newspaper editor*

BETTY DULLFEET, *his wife*

THE PASTOR

A LADY

ARTURO UI'S BODYGUARDS

DOGSBOROUGH'S MANSERVANT

REPORTERS

GUNMEN

GROCERS OF CHICAGO and CICERO

SYNOPSIS OF SCENES

The action of the play takes place in and around Chicago. The time is the early thirties.

PROLOGUE

SCENE 1: The Office of the Cauliflower Trust

SCENE 2: Before the Merchandise Mart

SCENE 3: Dogsborough's Saloon

SCENE 4: A Poolroom on 122nd Street

SCENE 5: Dogsborough's Country House

SCENE 6: City Hall

SCENE 7: Arturo Ui's Suite at the Mammoth Hotel

SCENE 8: The Office of the Cauliflower Trust

SCENE 9: A Street .

SCENE 10: A Court House

SCENE 11: Song of the Whitewash

SCENE 12: Dogsborough's Country House

The New York production had an act ending and an intermission at this point.

SCENE 13: Arturo Ui's Suite at the Mammoth Hotel

SCENE 14: A Garage

SCENE 15: Givola's Flower Store

SCENE 16: The Cicero Cemetery

SCENE 17: Arturo Ui's Bedroom at the Mammoth Hotel

SCENE 18: Convention Hall, Chicago

EPILOGUE

The Resistible Rise
of Arturo Ui

PROLOGUE

The BARKER *steps before the scene curtain which is covered with big headlines: NEWS ABOUT THE DOCK-CONSTRUCTION SCANDAL—HASSLE OVER OLD DOGSBOROUGH'S TESTAMENT AND CONFESSION—SENSATIONAL REVELATIONS AT THE GREAT WAREHOUSE FIRE TRIAL—GANGSTER ERNESTO ROMA MURDERED BY HIS FRIENDS—THE BLACKMAIL AND ASSASSINATION OF IGNATIUS DULLFEET—GANGSTERS CONQUER THE CITY OF CICERO.*

Honkytonk music offstage.

THE BARKER.
Ladies and gentlemen, we present today
The great historical gangster-play!
Learn all about blackmail and frameup! Further:
How to succeed in big business through murder.
—Good evening, sir. Put down that gun!
   Shut up, you guys! The show's begun!—
Hear all about old Dogsborough's confession!
Watch the resistible rise in the Depression
Of one Arturo Ui! The notorious
Trial of the warehouse fire! The mysterious
Dullfeet murder! Justice lies in coma!
Togetherness in gangsterdom! Who rubbed out Ernie
   Roma?

9

And in the grand finale of the show:
Crooks conquering the town of Cicero!
You'll see enacted by our finest actors
The underworld's most fabled malefactors!
All the rotten, ill-begotten heroes
Of the Thirties, here revealed as zeros!
Gangsters living, gangsters dying,
Gangsters selling, gangsters buying,
Gangsters born and gangsters made;
Some are gone and some have stayed.
So let's begin the big parade:
You've seen them all, but here you'll see the worst:
The grand old party boss, Dogsborough first!
   (*Old* DOGSBOROUGH *appears.*)
The hair is white but oh! the heart is black.
Pay your respects, you putrefying wreck!
   (*Old* DOGSBOROUGH *bows and withdraws.*)
Next on the bill, our flimflam artist
And here he comes—
   (GIVOLA *appears.*)
                —Givola the Florist!
Of all the silken, sly, insinuating Joes
He'd sell an icebox to the Eskimos!
He lubricates his lying lip with bile;
His crooked foot walks down a crooked mile!
   (GIVOLA *withdraws, limping.*)
Here's Ernie Roma, mouthpiece of the mob.
   (ROMA *appears.*)
Some piece of mouth. A hot malicious slob!
Drink, dope and death have set their marks on him
And all their ministers attend to him!
   (ROMA *withdraws.*)
Giri the Joker next, the Superclown!
Come take a bow, let's look you up and down!
   (GIRI *appears and waves a big hello.*)
His prime perversion, believe it or not,
Collecting the hats of the people he shot.
The cru'llest killer in Chicago town!

Go blow!
   (GIRI *withdraws angrily.*)
         And now with all his crimes full-blown,
Our top banana, the notorious
Gangster of all gangsters! The furious
Gods have sent him down to scourge us
For all our savage sins and urges,
Stupidities and apathies,
And cowardice, and here he is—
The troubler of this poor world's peace. O phooey!
The one and only great Arturo Ui!
   (UI *appears and walks along the footlights.*)
Look when he fawns he bites, and when he bites,
He rankles! Look you now! Give him more lights!
Now mark him well. You see as base a bird
As remember—the bastard!—Richard the Third!
   (UI *withdraws.*)
Not since the bloody War of Roses
Has mankind seen so many bloody noses,
Such grandiose and fulminating vices
Which justifies our slightly jacked-up prices.
What you will see is not entirely new
But half the world can testify it's true.
And if the other half does not remember them
The very butchers who dismembered them,
This bloody brood and all their high-class fellows,
Let's dig 'em up, let's cut 'em off the gallows!
Let's see them come alive in flesh again
Before the world does something rash again!
Great murderers, and that's a well-known fact,
Still do command from us too much respect!
But here's a show to end all gangster shows!
Enjoy it, folks, before the siren blows!

(*MUSIC SWELLS. A machinegun goes rat-tat-tat. The*
   BARKER *exits in a hurry.*)

SCENE ONE

Downtown Chicago. Enter five BUSINESSMEN, *leaders of the Cauliflower Trust.*

FLAKE.
Damn the Depression! It's as if Chicago,
Dear old Chicago, were a little girl
Who found her pockets full of holes one day
When Mother sent her out for morning milk.
She stands now in the gutter, wondering
Where Mother's last red cent is gone.
    CARUTHER.
                       Ted Moon
Invited eighty friends for Sunday brunch.
Had I but gone I would have found his brains
Upon the sidewalk, like a scrambled egg.
This change from boom to bust goes faster nowadays
Than you can blink an eye. Yet on the Seven Seas
The vegetable fleets come sailing as before.
To feed the customers.
    CLARK.
                  What customers?
    BUTCHER.
It's as if night had fallen one bright noon.
    MULBERRY.
Clive and Robber under the bailiff's hammer.
    CLARK.
Wheeler's fruit-business, older than the rocks
Gone into bankruptcy. Dick Havelock's
Garages closing down.
    CARUTHER.
               And where is Sheet?
    FLAKE.
Too busy to attend our conference.
Running from bank to bank to raise a loan.

CLARK.
What? Sheet's in trouble, too?
(*Pause.*)
                                    In other words:
The cauliflower business in this town
Is down the drain.
    BUTCHER.
                        Chin up, good gentlemen!
We're not yet dead and therefore still alive.
    MULBERRY.
Not to be dead is not the same as living.
    FLAKE.
You call this living?
    BUTCHER.
                            What's this pessimism?
The food business is fundamentally sound.
Chicago must be fed come hail or shine.
The city does not live by bread alone.
She needs her groceries, which we supply.
    CARUTHER.
How's business in the groceries?
    MULBERRY.
                                        It stinks.
Most customers buy half a cabbage head.
On credit, too, if they can only get it.
    CLARK.
Our cauliflower rots.
    FLAKE.
                        Oh, by the way,
There is a character waiting outside.
I wouldn't mention it except it's strange.
His name is Ui.
    CLARK.
                    The gangster?
    FLAKE.
                                    In person.
He smells a rat and, incidentally,
Brown-noses round for new connections,

Suggests he might persuade the groceries
To buy no cauliflower but from us.
If only to preserve their health. What's more,
He guarantees to double our grosses,
Because the grocers, Mr. Ui says,
Would rather buy a cabbage than a coffin.
 (*Uneasy laughter.*)
 CARUTHER.
What impudence!
 MULBERRY. (*With a hearty laugh.*)
                    Yes, Tommy-guns and hand-grenades!
A new approach to break down sales' resistance!
The word is out we do not sleep so well,
So in a hurry comes Arturo Ui
Off'ring his services, so here's the choice:
Salvation Army versus Ui. Well,
Where would you rather have your soup, my friends?
 CLARK.
You need a longish spoon to sup with Ui.
 CARUTHER.
Throw the bum out!
 MULBERRY.
                    But politely! Who knows
Which way the cookie crumbles.
 (*Laughter.*)
 FLAKE.
                    Gentlemen:
Butcher and I cooked up a little plan
To pull us through these deadly days of slump,
While we are all a little short on cash.
Let City Hall, grown fat on our taxes,
Give us a hand in our predicament
By granting us a loan for, shall we say,
Improving dock-facilities, to make
Our vegetables cheaper for the plebs.
Old Dogsborough, using his influence,
Could set it up. And what says Dogsborough?

BUTCHER.
Piss off, that's what he says. He wouldn't touch it
With a ten-foot pole.
FLAKE.
He would not touch it?
Damn his eyes, who made him ward boss on the docks?
CARUTHER.
For years I fattened his election funds!
MULBERRY.
He used to run Sheet's cafeteria
Before he switched to politics. And now?
Ingratitude thy name is Dogsborough!
All-seeing heaven, what a world is this?
People are short on cash but shorter still
On loyalty. Friends turning into foes,
And Yesmen shrieking "No sir!" as they come
Stampeding down the sinking ship like rats;
Like good old Dogsborough who coldly turns
His mighty shoulder. O morality,
Where art thou in this time of crisis, where?
CARUTHER.
I can't believe it about Dogsborough.
FLAKE.
What's his excuse?
BUTCHER.
"I wouldn't touch it, boys!
Foul fish, that's how your proposition stinks."
FLAKE.
What's fishy about building dock-facilities?
BUTCHER.
He doubts that we will ever build.
FLAKE.
For shame!
BUTCHER.
What? That we'll never build?
FLAKE.
No, that he doubts.
CLARK.
Let someone else arrange the loan.

BUTCHER.

Like who?

CLARK.

Well, get another wheelhorse . . .

MULBERRY.

Gouge or Slift.

BUTCHER.

There's no one like the good old Dogsborough.
That man is good.

CLARK.

For what?

BUTCHER.

He's honorable.

What's more, he's known as honorable.

FLAKE.

Balls!

BUTCHER.

Fact is he likes his reputation.

FLAKE.

So?

Fact is we want a loan from City Hall.
His reputation, well, that's his affair.

BUTCHER.

Is it indeed? No, I believe it's ours.
We need an honorable man to get
A loan without too many awkward questions.
The City Dads would be ashamed to ask
Old Dogsborough for vouchers or receipts.
They trust him. Men who ceased to trust in God
Do trust in him. Hard-boiled politicos
Who would not say hello to my attorney
Without consulting their attorneys first
Would put their last cent in the old man's purse.
Two hundred pounds of honesty he is.
The eighty winters of his spotless life
Have passed without a trace of graft. That man
Is worth his weight in gold to us. For when
He vouches for a loan, it's in the bag.

FLAKE.
Unfortunately, he won't vouch for us.
"The city is no pork barrel," he says.
  CLARK.
"Aye, let use keep our city clean, me boys!"
He sent Mike Glotz to jail for tax evasion.
"Conflict of interest" was his excuse.
Had Grisby fired for what? Embezzlement.
  CARUTHER.
No sense of humor. Find it quite revolting.
  MULBERRY.
He changes principles less frequently
Than shirts. For him the city isn't made
Of steel and stone where man eats fellow-man
Over a hunk of meat, the neighbor's job.
It's something Biblical and pastoral.
I never liked the man.
  CLARK.
                    No, in his heart
He never was a corporation man.
What's artichoke to him, or he to artichoke?
What does he know about the trucking business?
He never had to handle cauliflower
Except when it was plopped upon his plate.
As far as he's concerned our groceries
Can stink to heaven. Now he says "Piss off!"
For twenty years, or was it twenty-one,
We filled his coffers at election time.
Let him go to hell!
  BUTCHER.
                    No, let us go to him.
  FLAKE.
Clark made it clear he would not help us out.
  BUTCHER.
Clark also made it clear why that is so.
  CLARK.
He has no finer feelings for the trade.
Something is missing.

BUTCHER.
That's it! What is missing?
Understanding, that's what's missing!
Dogsborough simply can't imagine what
It feels to walk in, shall we say, our shoes.
How could we put him in our shoes, my friends?
Ay, there's the rub. What shall we do to him?
Teach him a lesson. 'Tis pity for the man,
But learn he must. Now listen to my plan.

(*A sign appears recalling certain historical events:
"1929–1932. WORLDWIDE SLUMP HITS GER-
MANY HARD. PRUSSIAN LANDOWNERS
ANGLE FOR GOVERNMENT SUBSIDY. AT-
TEMPTS SO FAR UNSUCCESSFUL."*

SCENE TWO

Before the Merchandise Mart. FLAKE *and* SHEET, *conversing.*

SHEET.
I've been running from Pillar to Post. Post
Had gone fishing, Pillar was in his bath.
You only see the backs of friends these days.
Brother, before he meets another brother,
Puts on a pair of shabby shoes to save
Himself from being hustled for a touch.
Old partners meeting by the Stock Exchange
Are so afraid of parting from a buck
They look the other way or else they call
Each other by imaginary names.
The whole damn town has sewed her pockets up.
FLAKE.
So how about my offer?
SHEET.
Ah! To sell

Or not to sell. You want the whole menu
And pay me with a tip. And want my thanks
On top of it. No, thank you very much.
Let me not tell you what I think of you.
    FLAKE.
You won't get more from anybody else.
    SHEET.
I would have thought that you, my dearest friend,
Might give me more.
    FLAKE.
                  Money is dear, you know.
    SHEET.
Dearest for those who need it and I do,
Which you know best, being my dearest friend.
    FLAKE.
You cannot hang on to your shipping line.
    SHEET.
Nor to my wife, perhaps. You know that, too.
    FLAKE.
                              So
Why don't you sell?
    SHEET.
               To buy one year's reprieve?
    FLAKE.
We'll gladly settle for a million.
A nice round figure like your wife's—
    SHEET.
                      No, thanks.
There's one thing though that baffles me completely.
Why do you want my company?
    FLAKE.
                    Because
The Trust would like to help you. Don't you see?
    SHEET.
I don't see it at all. I must be blind.
What happened to my eyes that I can't see
How all you people want to help me out
Instead of grabbing everything I own?

FLAKE.
This bitterness won't help you off the hook.
SHEET.
At least it will not help the hook, dear Flake.
(*Three men come slinking by:* ARTURO UI *the gangster,* ERNESTO ROMA *his sidekick, and a* BODYGUARD. *Passing* FLAKE, UI *stares at him as if expecting to be spoken to.* ROMA *turns angrily to* UI *as they leave.*)
Who's that?
FLAKE.
                    Ui the gangster.—Won't you sell?
SHEET.
He seemed so anxious to accost you.
FLAKE. (*With a nervous laugh.*)
                                        Sure.
He keeps pursuing us with propositions
Of how to dump our cauliflow'r with force.
There are so many men like Ui nowadays,
Infecting our town, a leprosy,
Chewing a little finger first, an arm,
A shoulder next. Nobody knows from where
They come. Some dark and stinky hole, I guess.
These robberies, this reign of threat and terror,
Blackmail and bloodbath, e'en assassination,
This most uncivil war with battle cries
Like "Stick 'em up!"—"Your money or your life!"
This pestilence—we ought to stamp it out.
SHEET. (*Looks at him sharply.*)
Be quick about it. It's contagious.
FLAKE.
                              Now
You think about the deal or else. . . .
SHEET. (*Steps back, studying* FLAKE.)
                                        It's true.
There is a similarity. To those
Who just walked by. It isn't very clear,
Something you feel but cannot see. It's like
A presence on the bottom of a pond,

Some green and gooey twigs that could be snakes,
But no, they're twigs. Or are they, Brother Flake?
You do resemble Ui. Don't be sore.
I see something I must have seen before
But did not understand about you, sir.
Say once again: "You think about the deal. . . ."
The voice is just the same. You'd better say:
"Go stick 'em up!" For that is what you mean.
I'll stick 'em up, Flake.
    (*Raises his hands.*)
                    Take my company.
And kick me in the balls for recompense.
Or kick me twice. And even better deal.
Or d'you prefer . . . ?
    FLAKE.
                  You're mad.
    SHEET.
                      I wish I were.

SCENE THREE

Back room in Dogsborough's saloon. DOGSBOROUGH *and* SON *behind the counter, rinsing glasses. Enter* BUTCHER *and* FLAKE.

    DOGSBOROUGH.
Wasting your time, me boys. I wouldn't touch it.
Foul fish, that's how your proposition stinks.
    YOUNG DOGSBOROUGH.
My father says it stinks.
    BUTCHER.
                Forget it, sir.
We asked a question and you answered No.
Okay, it's No.
    DOGSBOROUGH.
            I told you once before
I would not touch the case.

YOUNG DOGSBOROUGH.

My father says
He would not touch the case.
DOGSBOROUGH.

I know about
These so-called dock constructions.
YOUNG DOGSBOROUGH.

My father knows.
BUTCHER.
Well, it's been nice to see you, Dogsborough.
DOGSBOROUGH.
I hate to send you on your way, me boys.
The city is no pork barrel, you know,
For everyone to dip his fingers in.
Why, damn it all, you're in a healthy trade.
BUTCHER.
What did I tell you, Flake? You are a pessimist.
DOGSBOROUGH.
And pessimism is nothing less than treason.
You knife each other in the back, me boys.
What for? What's it you're selling? Cauliflow'r.
It's every bit as good as bread or meat.
Man doesn't live by bread and meat alone.
He's got to have his vegetables too.
Try serve a steak without a baked potato
And you'll offend the palate of the guest.
I know that temporarily some men
Are here and there a little short on cash.
They hesitate before they buy a shirt,
But they can sure afford a dime for groceries.
Prosperity is just around the corner.
Keep smiling, boys.
FLAKE.

Gee, Mr. Dogsborough!
It feels so good to hear you talk like that.
You give us hope.
BUTCHER.

It's most encouraging

To see you, sir, so full of confidence,
So steadfast in your vegetable faith.
Let me be frank. We are on business here.
No, not about the loan. You may relax.
It's something more agreeable, we hope.
The Trust had just discovered that in June
Some twenty years, a generation, passed
Since you, our trusted caterer, resigned
From one of our subsidiary firms,
To dedicate your life to public weal.
This town would not be quite the same without you
Nor we, the Trust, the same without the town.
I'm glad you find us fundamentally sound.
And so, to demonstrate on this occasion
Our high esteem and deep appreciation,
You hold a special niche in our hearts!
We passed a resolution yesterday
To offer you this fair portfolio,
Controlling shares in Sheet's old company,
Worth twice as much whene'er you wish to sell.
   (*Puts a portfolio of shares on the counter.*)
   DOGSBOROUGH.
Butcher, what are you up to?
   BUTCHER.

                              I'll be blunt.
A cauliflower has no bleeding heart,
Nor is the Trust exactly famous for
Its goody-goodness, oh but when we heard
Your thund'ring answer to our foolish plea—
To lobby for a loan from City Hall—
An answer honest as the day is long
And ruthless in its very rectitude,
So typical of grand old Dogsborough,
I must confess though with embarrassment,
Some people at the office wept aloud.
"Well, gentlemen," said one of us at last,—
Don't worry, Flake, I will not mention names—

"s we goofed." There was a sniffly pause,
"n we passed the resolution, sir.

DOGSBOROUGH.
Butcher and Flake, what is behind this, eh?

BUTCHER.
What do you think? The sign of our esteem.

FLAKE.
It is our joy to make this gift to you.
Ah, there you stand, the Watchdog of the Docks!
The very image of an Honest Abe,
Your name a household word, Boss Dogsborough!
A mighty man you are in your saloon,
Rinsing those glasses, nay, our very souls!
And yet you're poorer than your poorest guest.
'Tis very touching.

DOGSBOROUGH.
                    Don't know what to say.

BUTCHER.
Say nothing then. Put that packet away.
An honest man can use some extra cash.
Don't shake your snowy locks, for Lady Luck
Walks rarely down the path of righteousness.
You, too, young man. You have a golden name.
But who can eat his name? Go take the stuff.

DOGSBOROUGH.
Sheet's company!

FLAKE.
                    D'you see it over there?

DOGSBOROUGH.
I've seen it every day for twenty years.

FLAKE.
We thought of that.

DOGSBOROUGH.
                    And what will Sheet be doing?

FLAKE.
He switched to selling beer, I understand,
We fixed him up real nice.

BUTCHER.

It's settled then?

DOGSBOROUGH.
I sure appreciate the loving thought
Behind your gift but, surely, gentlemen,
There is no Santa Claus, and companies
Are not given away for free—

FLAKE.

Could be.
These stocks would come in handy to us, sir,
Now that the city loan has fallen through.

BUTCHER.
But oh, the market being as it is,
We couldn't liquidate them safely—

DOGSBOROUGH.

True.
That would be foolish. Now you're talking sense.
If only I were sure there are no strings
Attached.

FLAKE.

Oh no.

DOGSBOROUGH.

I used to work for Sheet.
I got me start, a two-bit kitcheneer.
If only I were sure you're shooting straight!
Have you two really given up the scheme
Of angling for a city loan?

FLAKE.

Scouts' honor.

DOGSBOROUGH.
I'd like to think it over. Well, my son,
That would be something for you, eh?
    (*To* FLAKE *and* BUTCHER.)

Me boys,
I thought I had your dander up, but no,
This time you brought a decent proposition.
    (*To* YOUNG DOGSBOROUGH.)
It pays to be an honest man, you see!

(*To* FLAKE *and* BUTCHER.)
And, like you say, he's nothing but a name.
My reputation is my capital.
When I am gone I'll leave him little else.
Honesty is rich legacy, but ah!
It cannot be insured against decay.
I've seen much evil in my time. Need always
Causes greed.
 BUTCHER.
     A stone would fall from our hearts
If you'd accept our present, Dogsborough.
The bitter aftertaste of our foolish plea
Would pass away. And in the future, sir,
We all could benefit from your advice
Of how to manage in these deadly days
Through honest trade. For in the future, sir,
It would be your trade, too. Yes, in the future, sir,
You too could be a cauliflower man.
 (DOGSBOROUGH *grasps his hand.*)
 DOGSBOROUGH.
I'll take your offer, Butcher and Flake.
 YOUNG DOGSBOROUGH.
Flake and Butcher, my father says he'll take.

(*A sign appears: JUNKERS PRESENT PRESIDENT
 HINDENBURG WITH COUNTRY ESTATE,
 FAMOUS BEAUTY SPOT AT NEUDECK, TO
 AROUSE HIS SYMPATHY FOR THEIR
 PLIGHT.*)

SCENE FOUR

Bookies' office on 122nd Street. ARTURO UI *and his sidekick* ERNESTO ROMA, *attended by* BODYGUARDS, *are
 listening to racing reports on the radio.—*DOCKDAISY,
 next to* ROMA.

Roma.
I wish you didn't mope around, Arturo!
Stop being such a melancholy babe!
Cast off thy unprevailing woes, my friend!
Snap out of idle reveries of which
The whole town's talking.

Ui. (*Bitterly.*)

Talking? Who's talking?
Noboby talks about me any more.
Yeh, fame is kinda shortlived in this burg!
"Whatever happened to Arturo Ui?"
Two months without a brawl, and twenty murders
All forgotten. Inside my flock o' buzzards, too.

(*Skipping through some newspapers.*)
When guns are silent, so's the goddamm Press!
And even if I do a coupla murders
I can't be sure it's gonna hit the front page.
It's influence what counts and not the act,
And influence depends on bank balance.
Sometimes I feel I wanna quit.

Roma.

Oh yeh?
The boys are getting pissed off on account
They're short on petty cash, and what is worse,
Inaction is demoralizing them.
The toughest mug gets easily corrupted
By having nothing but a beer bottle to shoot.
Their Lugers have their bowels full of wrath,
And they are ready mounted to let go
Their iron indignation on the world.
Arturo, I feel sorry for them guys.
I hesitate to face them in the hide-out.
I choke when I'm about to tell them, "Boys,
Get set for action in the morning." They
Just look at me with hangdog eyes and groan.
Your last idea was a cinch, Arturo.
I mean the grocery protection racket.
Why not get started now?

UI.

                         Not now. Not from
Below. It is too soon.

  ROMA.

                   "Too soon" is good.
Four months ago the cauliflower gents
Gave you the brushoff. So now you sit and brood.
Plans, plans! Half-assed attempts at action! Man,
Your visit to the Trust has broke your back.
Another thing that got under your skin,
The little holdup at the Corn Exchange
And how the cops behaved. . . .

  UI.

                          They shot at me!

  ROMA.
Two feet above your head.

  UI.

                     But even that
Was very rude of them. But for Dockdaisy here,
Who swore she spent the night with me—oh God!—
I would be up the river now for life.
Them judges got no sympathy for me.

  ROMA.
No cops will shoot to save a grocery.
For banks they'll shoot. So listen, let's begin
On 22nd Street. The windows smashed,
The vegetables sprayed with kerosene,
The fixtures hacked to pieces. Then we'll work
Our way down all the way to 7th Street.
And two days later Manuele Giri,
Carnation in his buttonhole, will pay
A visit to them crummy little stores,
And offer our protection free of charge,
Except for ten percent from off the top.

  UI.

                            No.
I gotta have protection first myself.
From cops and courts I gotta have protection

Before I can protect somebody else.
   (*Mournfully.*)
Gee, how I'd like a judge inside my pocket
By putting something in his pocket first!
Buy me a judge, or else I got no rights
And every time I wanna rob a bank
Some cheesy cop can shoot me full of holes.
   ROMA.
If that's the way you feel, send for Givola.
The Clubfoot has a mighty nose for dirt.
"There's something rotten in the State of Illinois,"
He says. He means the cauliflower boys.
There is a rumor they received a loan
From City Hall, arranged by Dogsborough.
And ever since there's gabbing on the grapevine
Of this and that, and something to be built
That wasn't built but shoulda been. It's strange.
Old Dogsborough would never touch a deal
That smells of graft. Here comes the horse's mouth.
Ragg from *The Star*. Hello, Ted, how's the press?
   RAGG. (*Somewhat drunk.*)
Hello, you two! Hi!, Roma! Ui, hello!
How's tricks in Philippi?
   UI.
                  Philippi who?
   RAGG.
Philippi was a place in Italy
Where once a famous army went to seed
Through easy living, inactivity,
And lack of exercise.
   UI.
                The hell with you!
   ROMA.
Go easy, Ted. Give us the dope about
The cauliflower loan.
   RAGG.
             What's that to you?
You're selling cauliflower now? I see!

You want a city loan yourselves! Go ask
Old Dogsborough. He'll grease the way for you.
    (*Imitating the old man.*)
"Should this fair flower of our city's trade,
So flourishing in ordinary times,
But threatened temporarily by drought
Wither and die?" No eye remained dry as
The old man spoke. The City Fathers were
So moved you'd think that cauliflower was
A piece of their anatomy. But ah!
It's hard to sympathize with tommy guns.
    (*The other* CUSTOMERS *laugh.*)
    ROMA.
Quit razzing him. He's feeling kinda blue.
    RAGG.
I'm not surprised. Givola's working for
Capone, I understand.
    DOCKDAISY.
                        Hey, that's a lie!
Leave my Giuseppe out of this, you pig!
    RAGG.
Dockdaisy dear!
    (*Introducing her.*)
                        The Clubfoot's bartered bride!
Assistant bride, no, fourth assistant bride
To one who rides through bloody constellations,
A third assistant planet, circling him—
    (*Points at* UI.)
A fading star of second-rate importance.
What an eclipse!
    DOCKDAISY.
                        Aw, shut yer dirty trap!
    RAGG.
No wreaths are woven by posterity
For killerdillers and their like, Arturo.
The fickle crowd turns to the latest thug.
Where are the goons of yesteryear? Who knows?
Their warrants gather dust in some archive.

"Have I not wounded you?"—"When?"—"Once ago."
"But all these wounds are long turned into scars,
And e'en the deepest scars do crumble into dust
With him that, bleeding, bore them once and died."—
"The good is oft interrèd with our bones;
You mean, the evil that we do will not
Survive us either?"—"No."—"Oh, cruel world!"
   (*Singing.*)
There was a little man,
He had a little plan.
His masters told him: Later!
He waited like a waiter. . . .
   UI. (*Bellowing.*)
Stop up his mouth!
   RAGG. (*Goes pale.*)
             No rough-house with the press!

   (*The* GUESTS *rise in alarm.*)

   ROMA. (*Hustling* RAGG *to the door.*)
You said enough. Get outa here and fast.
   RAGG. (*Backing out, very scared.*)
See you anon.

(*The place is getting quickly deserted. A shot Offstage.*
   UI *jumps.*)

   ROMA.
          Arturo, you're so nervous.
   UI.
These creeps, they talk to me like I was crap.
   ROMA.
Because you've been so very quiet lately.
   UI. (*Gloomily.*)
Where's Giri and the cauliflower guy?
   ROMA.
They should be here at 3 o'clock, he said.
   UI.
What's this about Givola and Capone?

ROMA.
Capone's been to his flower-store, that's all.
Nothing to it. Ordered a bunch of wreaths.
UI.
A bunch of wreath? For who?
ROMA.

                              I wouldn't know.
But not for us.
UI.

                    I'm going home.
ROMA.

                              Arturo!
Tonight you got the heebie-jeebies, Chief.
Nobody cares enough to bump you off.
UI.
They don't? You see? That's what I mean, Ernesto.
They're giving more respect to horse manure.
I know that life's no bed of roses now,
But Mr. Clubfoot takes a lam, the fink!
And now he feasts, mousing the flesh of friends!
I'm gonna take him for a ride, Ernesto,
As soon as I get credit for a car.
ROMA.
Giri!

(*Enter* EMANUELE GIRI *with a shabby character,* BOWL.)

GIRI.
Boss, here's the man. His name is Bowl.
ROMA.
You work for Mr. Sheet?
BOWL.

                         I used to work,
I used to be his chief cashier, sir. . . .
GIRI.
He hates the smell of cauliflower now.
A very ancient fishlike smell it is.

BOWL.
. . . Until a week ago when Dogsborough,
That dirty dog . . .
   UI. (*Quickly.*)

                       What's this with Dogsborough?
   ROMA.
What have you got to do with Dogsborough?
   GIRI.
That's why I brought him here.
   BOWL.

                            He had me fired.
   ROMA.
From Sheet's company?
   BOWL.

                    His own! It's now his own!
Since last September. . . .
   ROMA.

                Wow!
   GIRI.

                    Sheet's company
Was given by the Trust to Dogsborough.
Butcher arranged the transfer of the shares
And Bowl was present when the deal was signed.
   UI.
So what?
   BOWL.

      So what? A crying shame it is.
   GIRI.
Boss, don't you see the light?
   BOWL.

                  Old Dogsborough
Arranged a city loan to save the Trust.
   GIRI.
While secretly he sat inside the Trust.
   UI. (*Begins to dawn on him.*)
He did? But that's corruption! Jesus Christ!
   BOWL.
The loan was paid officially to Sheet

That he improve his dock facilities.
I signed for it. I didn't sign for Sheet.
As people think. I signed for Dogsborough.
And all the money went through Dogsborough
Straight to the Cauliflower Trust.
   GIRI.
                               Bingo!
We hit the jackpot, Boss. Oh, Dogsborough!
Ye rusty shop-sign for a rotten town!
Ye honest-to-goodness shaker of hands!
Ye clean-in-the nose unbribable sage!
   BOWL.
He had me fired for an oversight
Which he then chose to call embezzlement!
And he himself is worse than . . .
   ROMA.
                          Simmer down!
You're not the only one whose blood is boiling.
So what's the good word, Boss?
   UI.
                      Will he repeat it
Under oath?
   GIRI.
         He sure will.
   UI.
                 Give him good watch.
   (*Starts out grandly.*)
Come, Roma, let us blow! I smell a deal.
   (*Exits quickly, followed by* ROMA *and* BODYGUARDS.)
   GIRI.
Some ball you started rolling.
   BOWL.
                   Where's my cut?
   GIRI.
Relax. I know the Boss. He wouldn't screw you.
You'll get it sure as hell what's coming to you.

(*A sign appears: FALL, 1932. NAZI PARTY FACES*

*FINANCIAL RUIN AND DISINTEGRATION.
HITLER DESPERATE TO SEIZE POWER.
HINDENBURG REFUSES TO SEE HIM.*)

SCENE FIVE

Dogsborough's country house. DOGSBOROUGH *and* SON.

DOGSBOROUGH.
Oh, why did I accept this country house?
To take the shares they gave me as a sign
Of their esteem, a kind of gift, was quite
Above reproach.
YOUNG DOGSBOROUGH.
                    Oh, absolutely, Father.
DOGSBOROUGH.
Nor was there anything objectionable
About my sponsoring a city loan
When on my very skin I felt a threat
To that fair flower of our city's trade,
The cauliflower. Oh, but it was wrong
To take this house while recommending help
To City Hall in favor of a cause
Which secretly was also mine.
YOUNG DOGSBOROUGH.
                            Yes, Father.
DOGSBOROUGH.
It was a fault, or could be so construed.
We have been hooked, my son.
YOUNG DOGSBOROUGH.
                        Yes, Father, hooked.
DOGSBOROUGH.
Those shares were like the peanuts in a bar
That all the barmen offer free of charge
To satisfy the client's hunger cheaply
But make him thirsty for expensive booze.
    (*Pause.*)

I do not like the news that City Hall
Might probe into the dock construction deal.
The loan's been spent. Yes, Clark took some of it,
And Butcher took, and Flake, and God forgive,
I also took and so far not a pound
Of concrete bought. The only good thing is
I did not beat the drum about the deal,
At Sheet's request. Thus no outsider knows
That I'm the owner of his company.

   MANSERVANT. (*Entering.*)
Mr. Butcher's on the phone.
   DOGSBOROUGH.

                      You take it, son.
(YOUNG DOGSBOROUGH *exits with* MANSERVANT.
CHURCH BELLS from a distance.)
Butcher is on the line! I wonder why.
   (*Looks out of the window.*)
Oh, why did I accept this country house??
The silver poplars were the cause of it.
Ah, and the view. The lake looks just like silver
Before it's beaten to a dollar piece.
And oh! the joy of living in a place
Without the sour smell of beer. And then
It's very nice to look upon the pines,
Especially the top of pines. There is
A dusk about them, dusty gray and green.
Their trunks are of the color of my apron
Which in the old days I would often wear
When tapping beer. But what was most decisive
Were the poplars. The poplars were the cause.
Today is Sunday. The church bells sound so
Peaceful. Ah, if the world were not so full
Of human wickedness.

   YOUNG DOGSBOROUGH. (*Returning.*)
                  Dad, Butcher says that
City Hall decided to investigate
The dock construction deal. You're feeling ill?

DOGSBOROUGH.

My camph—or—bottle. What's Butcher gonna do?

YOUNG DOGSBOROUGH.

He's coming here.

DOGSBOROUGH.

      I will not see him, son.

I don't feel well. My heart . . .

 (*Rises grandly.*)

          I'm innocent,

In this affair. I will have none of it.

For sixty years I walked the straight and narrow.

I've not a thing in common with these crooks.

Which everybody knows about me, son.

YOUNG DOGSBOROUGH.

Yes, Father. Are you feeling better now?

MANSERVANT. (*Entering.*)

A Mr. Ui's here.

DOGSBOROUGH.

     The gangster?

MANSERVANT.

         Must be him.

I saw his picture in the Sunday *News*.

He says that Mr. Clark has sent him here.

DOGSBOROUGH.

Well, throw him out! Who sent him? Clark, you say?

Well, I'll be damned!! Go set the dogs on him!

  (*Enter* ARTURO UI *and* ERNESTO ROMA.)

UI.

Say, Mr. Dogsborough—

DOGSBOROUGH.

     Get out!

ROMA.

        Tsk. Tsk.

Let's not be hasty, sir. Let us be friendly.

It's Sunday, after all.

DOGSBOROUGH.

           I say, get out.

YOUNG DOGSBOROUGH.

My father says, get out.

  ROMA.

            Say it again.

I've heard it said before. What else is new?

  UI. (*Stubbornly.*)

Say, Mr. Dogsborough—

  DOGSBOROUGH. (*To his son.*)

              Go get the cops!

Where are the servants?

  ROMA.

           Don't leave, sonnyboy.

Look out the window. You've got company.

My two assistants waiting in the yard.

They might misunderstand you if you split.

  DOGSBOROUGH.

So. Violence.

  ROMA.

       Oh no. No violence.

Just emphasis.

          (*Silence.*)

  UI.

       Sir, Mr. Dogsborough!!

I am aware you don't know me from nothing,

Or maybe just from hearsay which is worse.

You see before you, sir, a man misunderstood,

And almost done to death by sland'rous tongues,

His name besmirched by envy, and his dreams

Misrepresented by a world replete

With Jews and bicyclists. It only was

A little over fourteen years ago

That me—that I—the simple son of Brooklyn

Came west without a job, a country boy

Who cried, "Chicago, I will lick you yet!"

I didn't altogether fail, although

I did it all alone but for the help
Of seven solid buddies standing by
Without a pot to piss in, like myself,
But firm in our determination, sir,
To carve ourselves that little piece of goose
Which God Almighty cooks for every Christian.
The tribe of seven's grown to thirty now
And there'll be more of us, I guarantee.
You ask yourself, I guess: "What's Ui want?"
Not much. One thing, that's all I want from you.
I don't want to be misconstrued no more,
And treated like some greaseball racketeer,
Or whate'er else they call me in this town.
I want respect.
   (*Clears his throat.*)
                  At least from the police,
Whom I have always so appreciated,
And that's the reason I am standing here,
And begging you, and I don't like to beg,
To say a little word on my behalf
Whenever, God forbid, the heat is on.
   DOGSBOROUGH. (*Incredulously.*)
Are you suggesting I should vouch for you?
   UI.
Yeh, when the heat is on. And that depends
On how we make out with the groceries.
   DOGSBOROUGH.
What interest d'you have in groceries?
   UI.
I sucked pimento with my mother's milk!
And I'm determined to protect the Grocers.
From force and violence. With force and violence
If necessary.
   DOGSBOROUGH.
                  As far as I can tell
No one is threatening the grocers now.
   UI.
Now's maybe right. But I can see ahead.

I ask you, sir, how long in such a town,
Where all the cops are lazy and corrupt,
Before the grocers cease to sell their stuff
In peace? Who knows but maybe by tonight
Some little stores will all be smashed to bits,
Their cashbox cracked by ruthless mobster hands.
I think the grocers would enjoy protection.
Against a modest fee.

    DOGSBOROUGH.

                      I don't agree.

    UI.

Well, Mr. Dogsborough, that only proves
They don't know what the fuck is good for them.
That's possible. A grocer is a jerk.
He's diligent but limited up here.
Honest as day but farsighted he ain't.
He needs a leadership that's really strong.
He don't know nothing, I am sad to say,
Of loyalties he owes to those to whom
He owes his very life. I mean the Trust.
The Trust will also need protection, sir.
The Great Collector I will be to them.
"Prompt payment on delivery or else!
The days of swindle-sheets are over, men!
Correct accounts or close the store. Settle
The score with everyone who cheats! The weak
Fall by the road, but that's the law of nature."

    DOGSBOROUGH.

Dear sir, the Trust is none of my concern.
I think you've brought your most remarkable
Ideas to the wrong address.

    UI.

                      Did I?

We'll talk about that later, Dogsborough.
It's brass knuckles they need inside the Trust
And thirty trigger-artists led by me!

    DOGSBOROUGH.

I doubt if any reputable firm

Would swap their typewriters for tommy guns.
But then I wouldn't know about those things.
I'm not a member of the Trust.
   Ui.

                        You're not?
We'll talk about that later, Dogsborough.
I guess what worries you is thirty guys
Armed heavily with hardware, walking in
And out the Head Office. Who guarantees
They won't annex the joint. Please relax.
The answer's simple. He who has the cash,
Who dishes out the payroll is the boss.
You are the boss. How could I boss you 'round?
If that's what worries you. I wouldn't, sir,
Not if I felt like it, which I do not,
And didn't so respect you, which I do.
You have my word. What am I, after all?
How big a following do I command?
I've twenty boys, if twenty, maybe less.
You know that some already finked on me?
You gotta help me, sir, or I am through.
It is your duty as a human being
To protect me from my mortal enemies
And, Mamma mia, maybe from my friends.
The work of fourteen years is now at stake.
So I appeal to you as man to man—
   Dogsborough.
And let me tell you, man to man, what I
Propose to do. I'm calling the police.
   Ui.
The who?
   Dogsborough.
          You heard me. The police.
   Ui.
                        You mean
To tell me you refuse to help me, as
A human being?
   (*Screaming.*)

Then I demand you help
Me as a crook. Because that's what you are!
I've got the goods on you! I've got the proof!
You're mixed up in the dock-construction scandal
Which is about to pop! You own Sheet's company!
I'm warning you, don't drive me to extremes!
My patience is exhausted! City Hall
Could be persuaded to investigate!

DOGSBOROUGH.

For sixty years I walked the straight and narrow!

ROMA.

You made a little detour at the end.

DOGSBOROUGH.

I have no knowledge of these slipp'ry deals!

ROMA.

Let the inquiry tell . . .

DOGSBOROUGH.

There won't be one!
My friends would never . . .

UI.

Friends? You got no friends!
You had them yesterday! You got no friends today!
Tomorrow you'll have only enemies!
If anyone can save you, then it's me,
Arturo Ui, me, me, me, me, me!

DOGSBOROUGH.

There will be no investigation, sir!
They couldn't do it t' me! My hair is white!

UI.

Which is about the only thing that's white
About you, man. So, listen, Dogsborough—

(*Tries to grasp his hand.*)

Now use your head and let me save your life!
Give me the green light, sir, and I will slug
Whoever tries to touch a single hair
Of yours. Dogsborough, help me, please, this once!
If you and me don't come to no arrangement,
How could I ever face the gang again?

(*Weeps.*)

DOGSBOROUGH.
Never! I'd go to rack and ruin first
Before I make a deal with you, Ui.

UI.
In that case I am through. I know I am.
I'm forty now and still a nobody.
You gotta help me.

DOGSBOROUGH.
                        No!

UI.
                              I'm warning you!
I can demolish you!

DOGSBOROUGH.
                        As long as I can breathe,
You'll never touch the cauliflower trade!

UI. (*With dignity.*)
Oh, very well, then, Mr. Dogsborough.
I'm forty now and you are pushing eighty.
With some assistance from Almighty God
I'm going to outlive you, sir. With me
It's cauliflower now! or bust. One day
The vegetable business shall be mine!

DOGSBOROUGH.
Never!

YOUNG DOGSBOROUGH.
        My father says, never.

UI.
                              Roma,
We're leaving.
(*Bows formally and leaves with* ERNESTO ROMA.)

DOGSBOROUGH.
                  Air! Fresh air! Oh, what a mess!
Oh, why did I accept this country house?
But, son, they wouldn't dare investigate me!
For if they do I'm finished.

YOUNG DOGSBOROUGH.
                              Yes, you are.

MANSERVANT. (*Entering.*)
A Mr. Goodwill, sir, from City Hall.
Accompanied by Mr. Gaffles.
DOGSBOROUGH.

Oh?

(*Enter* GOODWILL *and* GAFFLES.)

GOODWILL.
Hello, Dogsborough.
DOGSBOROUGH.

Goodwill! Gaffles! Hello!
What's new in town?
GOODWILL.

Nothing good, I'm afraid.
Was that Arturo Ui?
DOGSBOROUGH. (*With a forced smile.*)
Ui himself.
Came barging in, the brazen thug, with some
Demented plan. I threw him out, of course.
"Not my idea of a guest
On this our holy day of rest."
GOODWILL.
No guest on any day. Well, Dogsborough,
It is in ill wind that has blown us here.
The cauliflower loan . . .
DOGSBOROUGH. (*Stiffly.*)

And what about it?
GAFFLES.
The shit has hit the fan, to put it mildly.
Last night, in City Hall, some councilman,
Tipped off anonymously, I suppose,
Did call it fishy. . . .
DOGSBOROUGH.

Fishy?
GOODWILL.

Rest assured.
The majority resented the expression.

A miracle they didn't come to blows.
They stomped and romped and screamed: "Withdraw!!
    Withdraw!
The loan had Mr. Dogsborough's approval!
How dare you call it fishy, gentlemen?
If that is fishy, how about the Bible?"
That did it, Dogsborough. It always does.
The meeting ended honoring you—

DOGSBOROUGH.

                           Ah!

GAFFLES.

When we demanded full investigation,
To demonstrate our confidence in you,
The opposition backed down and declared
They wanted none of it, the craven fools!
Your friends, however, pressing their advantage
And anxious to defend your name against
The very slightest breath of scandal—

DOGSBOROUGH.

                           Ah?

GAFFLES.

Cried out, "Dogsborough isn't just a name,
Not just a man. He is an institution!"
That brought the house down.

DOGSBOROUGH.

                         Ahh!

GAFFLES.

                    And then the vote:

Investigation!

DOGSBOROUGH.

        Investigation?

GOODWILL.

The hearing will be headed by O'Casey.
The Trust, we understand, is not involved.
The loan was given to Sheet's company,
So I believe it would be best if you
Would find a man who has your confidence,

A reputable man, non-partisan,
To clarify this rotten mess.
  DOGSBOROUGH.
                           I see.
  GOODWILL.
Church bells! Peace! What more can a man wish for?
Why don't you show us 'round your country house?
  GAFFLES. (*Laughing.*)
No dock construction to disturb his rest.
  DOGSBOROUGH.
Come, friends, I'll find that man as you suggest.

(*They walk out slowly.*)

*A sign appears: JANUARY, 1933: HINDENBURG
NIXES HITLER AS HEAD OF GOVERNMENT.
AGING   PRESIDENT   THREATENED   BY
PROBE. MISAPPROPRIATION OF FUNDS?*

SCENE SIX

City Hall, FLAKE, BUTCHER, CLARK, MULBERRY, CA-
  RUTHER *on one side. On the other side*, DOGS-
  BOROUGH, *chalk-white in the face, with* O'CASEY,
  GAFFLES *and* GOODWILL.—REPORTERS.

  BUTCHER. (*In a low voice.*)
What takes Ui so long?
  MULBERRY.
                      He's bringing Sheet.
Unless they couldn't come to an agreement.
Sheet's got to testify that he is still
The owner of the shipping line.
  CARUTHER.
                      Poor Sheet!
No gravy train for him to walk in here
And publicly admit that he's a crook.

FLAKE.
He'll never do it.
BUTCHER
                    Yes, he will.
CLARK.
                              He must.
FLAKE.
Why should he take the rap and go to jail
For five long years?
CLARK.
                    There's plenty dough in it
For him, and Mabel Sheet loves luxury.
Even today he's wild about his Mabel.
And as for jail, he'll never see the in-
Side of a cell. Leave it to Dogsborough.

(*CRIES OF NEWSVENDORS outside. A* REPORTER
    rushes in with a newspaper.)

GAFFLES. (*Reading.*)
Sheet's dead. Found dead. In his hotel. Oh dear.
A ticket in his pants for Santa Fé.
BUTCHER.
Dead?
O'CASEY. (*Reading.*)
    Murdered.
MULBERRY.
                Oh.
FLAKE. (*In a low voice.*)
                    I guess he wouldn't do it.
GAFFLES.
Dogsborough, are you ill?
DOGSBOROUGH. (*With difficulty.*)
                              Sir, it will pass.
O'CASEY.
The death of Sheet—
CLARK.
                    The unexpected death
Of Sheet deals quite a blow to this inquiry.

O'CASEY.
The unexpected often comes expected.
One often does expect the unexpected.
That's life for you. But here I am, good friends,
All ready, set and go with all my questions.
I hope you won't refer them back to Sheet,
For Sheet is very silent since tonight,
According to the papers.
    MULBERRY.
                          What d'you mean?
The loan was granted to Sheet's company.
Or was it not?
    O'CASEY.
                  What I would like to know:
Who is this company?
    FLAKE. (*In a low voice.*)
                        A funny question.
What's he got up his sleeve?
    CLARK. (*Ditto.*)
                           I wouldn't know.
    O'CASEY.
Is anything the matter, Dogsborough?
Is it the air?
    (*To the others.*)
                  It seems unfair to me
That Sheet who'll soon be shovelled under earth
Should have to bear this other kind of dirt
As well. And I suspect . . .
    CLARK.
                        It would be wise
If you did not suspect so much, O'Casey.
We have some laws against malicious slander.
    MULBERRY.
What are these innuendoes, gentlemen?
Dogsborough's picked a man to clarify
The situation. Let us wait for him.
    O'CASEY.
He takes so long. And when he comes, I hope,
He will not only talk about poor Sheet.

FLAKE.
We hope he'll tell the truth and nothing else.
O'CASEY.
Ah then, he must be a most honorable man,
Which would be very nice and quite a change.
I hope you picked a good man, Dogsborough.
CLARK. (*Sharply.*)
He's what he is, okay? And here he comes.

(*Enter* ARTURO UI *and* ERNESTO ROMA, *attended by*
BODYGUARDS.)

UI.
Hello, Clark. Hello, Dogsborough. Hello.
CLARK.
Hello, Ui.
UI.
            So what you wanna know?
O'CASEY. (*To* DOGSBOROUGH.)
Is that your man?
CLARK.
                    Sure. Why not, gentlemen?
Isn't he good enough?
GOODWILL.
                    But, Dogsborough,
You cannot mean it.

(*Uproar among the* REPORTERS.)

O'CASEY.
                Order!
A REPORTER.
                        It's Ui!

(*Laughter.* O'CASEY *bangs his gavel, restoring order.
He studies* UI's BODYGUARDS.)

O'CASEY.
Who are these creatures?

UI.

                    Friends.

O'CASEY.

                              And who is that?

UI.

My social secret'ry, Ernesto Roma.

GAFFLES.

Good Dogsborough, you can't be serious.

(DOGSBOROUGH *is silent*.)

O'CASEY.

Silence most eloquent.

   (*To* UI.)

                              So you're the man
Who has Dogsborough's confidence, and now
Would like to have ours, too. Where are the contracts?

UI.

What kinda contracts?

O'CASEY.

                              Which the shipping line
Supposed to've signed with certain building firms
In reference to dock facilities.

UI.

I don't know nothing about contracts.

O'CASEY.

                                        No?

CLARK.

You mean they don't exist?

O'CASEY. (*Quickly*.)

                              You have seen Sheet—

UI. (*Shakes his head*.)

No.

O'CASEY.

   Are you sure you haven't seen him, sir?

UI. (*Flares up*.)

Whoever says that I've been seeing Sheet
Is nothing but a liar.

O'CASEY.
                        Pardon me.
I thought you might have seen him. After all
You studied this here case.
    UI.
                              And I did, too.
    O'CASEY.
And was it fruitful, your investigation?
    UI.
You bet your ass.
    O'CASEY.
                    Well, tell us, Mr. Ui.
    UI.
It wasn't easy to establish th' truth.
And pleasant it is not. When Mr. D.
Persuaded me to serve the city by
Inquiring into what the cat brought in,
Concerning certain city funds, consisting
Of us, the U.S. taxpay'rs' hard-earned cents,
Well, I discovered to my greatest shock:
Those funds were misabused. Fact Number One.
Fact Number Two: who misabused them, eh?
Here, too, my efforts met with great success.
The guilty party, may he rest—
    O'CASEY.
                                    Who's he?
    UI.
Why, Sheet.
    O'CASEY.
                Ah, silent Sheet, unholy Sheet
The Sheet you have not seen at all, at all.
    UI.
What are you looking at me for like that?
Get Sheet up here.
    O'CASEY.
                    He's dead. Or didn't you know?
    UI.
He's dead? I spent the night in Cicero.
With Roma here. That's why I didn't know.

(*Pause.*)

ROMA.
I call that strange. You think it's accidental?
To die just now . . .
   UI.
                          That was no accident.
His suicide's the consequence of crime,
Which in his case was something quite enormous.
   O'CASEY.
Except it was no suicide.
   UI.
                        What else?
Of course we spent the night in Cicero.
We know from nothing, but this much I know,
Which must be clear to all you guys by now:
That Sheet who seemed an honorable man
Was nothing but a racketeer.
   O'CASEY.
                           I see.
Sheet's kicked the bucket. Let us kick him, too,
While he is down. Let's cut him up with words
Now that he's dead and can't defend himself,
Cut down by something deadlier than words.
But now to you, dear Dogsborough . . .
   DOGSBOROUGH.
                          To me?
   BUTCHER. (*Sharply.*)
What do you want from Dogsborough?
   O'CASEY.
                          Not much.
Judging from Mr. Ui's explanations,
Unless I'm much mistaken, which I doubt,
The loan was given to a company
Which then embezzled it. So there remains
A final question to be answered here.
Who is this company? They call it Sheet's,
But, gentlemen, what's in a name, I ask?

Did it indeed belong to Sheet? He could
Undoubtedly enlighten us, but Sheet
Can no longer discuss his earthly goods,
Not since our Mr. Ui spent the night
In Cicero. So here's what we must ask:
Who owns this company, not what it's called;
Who was the real boss when the fraud was done?
Dogsborough, what is your opinion?

DOGSBOROUGH.

                                Mine?

O'CASEY.

Could it be you who sat behind the desk,
When certain contracts which were to be honored
Were, shall we say, dishonored . . .

GOODWILL.

                              Are you mad?

DOGSBOROUGH.

                                      I . . .

O'CASEY.

And on that earlier occasion here,
When you described in such a quiv'ring voice
How hard it is to be a cauliflower,
Insisting we assist that holy flower,
Did you not speak as secret sympathizer
For the cauliflower cause?

BUTCHER.

                         Now that's enough!

Or don't you see he's sick?

CARUTHER.

                         An old man, too!

FLAKE.

His snowy locks should tell you, gentlemen,
There can't be any evil in his heart.

ROMA.

Where is your proof, I ask?

O'CASEY.

                        Well, as for proof . . .

UI.
A little quiet, please. Let's have some order.
    GAFFLES. (*Loudly.*)
For God's sake, Dogsborough, speak up, speak up!
    A BODYGUARD. (*A sudden yell.*)
Shut up, you guys! The Boss wants quiet here!

(*Sudden silence.*)

UI.
What makes me mad in this most shameful hour,
If I may say so, is the spectacle
Of seeing this old gentleman abused,
His best friends clamming up, just standing by,
Nobody speaking up for him. So this
I gotta say: Sir, Mr. Dogsborough,
I do believe in you. I ask you guys,
Is this what guilt looks like? Is this the face
That could have maybe launched a thousand tricks?
If that's the case, I couldn't tell no more
If black is black and vice versa. So
We've gone too far if that's how far we go!
    CLARK.
The old man is above suspicion, men!
You dare suspect him of corruption, sir?
    O'CASEY.
And worse than that. Abuse of public trust.
Deceit and theft. Thus I accuse him now:
That shipping line we've heard so much about
Belonged to him when all that fraud was done.
    MULBERRY.
Liar!
    UI.
    I'd put my right hand in the fire
For Dogsborough! Go ask the city, men!
Find me a single solitary joker
Who calls him crooked!

A REPORTER. (*To another* REPORTER *entering.*)
                    Dogsborough accused
Of graft.
   SECOND REPORTER.
           Who's next, Abe Lincoln?
   MULBERRY and FLAKE.

                              Where's your witness?
Witness!
   O'CASEY.
           Witness? It's witnesses you want?
Smith, has he come? I think he's just arrived.

(SMITH, *a clerk, has gone to the door and signals someone outside. Everybody looks at the door. Brief
pause. A series of shots. Pandemonium. The* RE-
PORTERS *run out.*)

   THE REPORTERS.
Outside the building . . . Where? . . . Machine-gun
   fire. . . .
What's your witness's name, O'Casey?
   O'CASEY. (*Goes to the door.*)

                              Bowl.
   (*Yelling.*)
Come in here.
   A REPORTER.
           Tough shit. Ui rides again.
   THE CAULIFLOWER PEOPLE.
What's going on?—Someone's been shot.—Good God.
—Where? . . . On the steps? . . .
   BUTCHER. (*To* UI.)

                              More monkey business, eh?
We're parting company. . . .
   UI.

                    Yeh?
   O'CASEY.

                              Bring him in!

(A POLICEMAN *brings in a body.*)
It's Bowl. I do regret, but, gentlemen,
He seems unable now to testify. . . .
Meeting adjourned.

(*He exits quickly. The* POLICEMAN *carries* BOWL'S *body
into a corner. Tumult.*)

DOGSBOROUGH. (*To* GAFFLES.)
                    Please get me out of here.

(GAFFLES *walks out without answering. Tumult grow-
ing.*)

UI. (*Jumps up.*)
Murder! Butchery! Blackmail! Robbery! Fraud!
Guns chattering in public places! Men
Going about their peaceful occupation,
Solid citizens entering City Hall
To testify, mowed down in broadest daylight!
What are the City Dads doing about it?
Nothing! These so-called honorable men
Are busy spinning shady business plans
And shafting honest people in the back
Instead of giving them protection.
    A BODYGUARD.
                            Hear! Hear!
    UI.
But truth is marching on! Nothing will stop it!
Not all them scaly bums who got the nerve
To sling their mud upon them snowy locks
Where all suspicion crumbles into dandruff!
Dogsborough is the father of Chicago!
Sage of the Waterfront! Not just a name,
Not just a man! No, he's an institution!
Whoever is attacking him—or me—
Attacks the town, the state, the Constitution!
    (*Strides up to* DOGSBOROUGH, *to grasp his hand.*)

Congratulations, Mr. Dogsborough!
I like things clean-cut, and you made your choice!
It's this way and no other. I rejoice!

(*A sign appears: JANUARY 31, 1933: HINDENBURG
YIELDS TO HERR HITLER. FUEHRER TO
HEAD NEW GOVERNMENT. GRAFT IN-
QUIRY CALLED OFF.*)

SCENE SEVEN

Ui's suite at the Mammoth Hotel. Two BODYGUARDS
enter with a dilapidated ACTOR. *In the background,*
GIVOLA.

FIRST BODYGUARD. Here's the actor, Chief, but it's
okay, he's unarmed.

SECOND BODYGUARD. He ain't the pistol-packing type
except he's loaded, so he can do his recitations in the
joint around the corner, which is about the only place he
can recite these days and only when the customers are
also loaded. But he's supposed to be real good. He does
them classics.

UI. So listen. I've been informed that my pronounci-
ation ain't quite perfect. Now it's getting to be unavoid-
able that I should utter a few words here and there in
public, especially political-type words, so I wanna take
lessons in speech-making. Also, how to make an entrance.

THE ACTOR. Yes, sir.

UI. Get the mirror. (*One of the* BODYGUARDS *brings a
large standing mirror.*) Let's start with the walking.
How d'you guys walk around in the theater or the opera?

THE ACTOR. I understand. You must be referring to
the classical style. Julius Caesar, Hamlet, Romeo et
cetera. Mr. Ui, you've come to the right man. Maloney
can teach you the grand manner in ten minutes. Gentlemen, you see a tragic case before you. Shakespeare's been

my undoing. The English playwright, you know. If it weren't for the Bard, I'd be playing on Broadway today. Ah, the tragedy of an actor! My last engagement was suddenly terminated when this director said to me: "Stop chewing the scenery, Maloney. We're doing H. Ibsen, not Shakespeare. Look at the calendar, Maloney, this is 1912!"—"Art knows no calendar!" says I. "And I'm an artist." Ah yes.

GIVOLA. Seems to me you've got the wrong man, Chief. He is a has-been.

UI. We'll see about that. Walk around like you're supposed to walk in this Shakespeare. (*The* ACTOR *walks around.*) That's good.

GIVOLA. Chief, you can't walk around like that in front of grocers. It's unnatural.

UI. What's that mean, unnatural? No human being behaves natural these days. When I walk into that meeting tomorrow I don't want to look natural. I want them to notice that I'm walking in. (*Imitates the* ACTOR'S *walk.*)

THE ACTOR. Hold your head up! (UI *obeys.*) Let your toes touch the ground first. (UI *obeys.*) Good. Excellent. You have natural talent. Except you don't know what to do with your hands. Wait a moment. It might be best if you placed them in front of your genitals. (UI *obeys.*) Not bad. Spontaneous yet stylish. But the head's got to go up, Mr. Ui. That's it. I think the walk will do very nicely for your purposes. Anything else you wish to learn?

UI. How d'you stand in public?

GIVOLA. Put two musclemen behind you and you'll be standing fine.

UI. Bullshit. When I stand up, I want people to look at me, not the guys behind me. Correct me if I'm wrong. (*Strikes various poses, folding his arms, etc.*)

THE ACTOR. It's a possibility but it's a trifle common. You don't want to look like a hairdresser, do you, Mr. Ui? Cross your arms this way. (*Crosses his arms so that*

his hands are visible as they press on the upper arms.)
A minute change but it does make an enormous differ-
ence, doesn't it? Compare it yourself in the mirror, Mr.
Ui.

(UI *rehearses crossing his arms in front of the mirror.*)

UI.
That's good.
    GIVOLA.
                But what's it for, Chief? To impress
The high-hats in the Trust?
    UI.
                        Naturally not.
How come it's not self-evident to you
I'm doing it for all them little people?
Now Clark, for instance, from the Trust, he makes
A mighty fine impression. Who's it for?
I ask. His kinda stuffshirts? No, Givola.
His bank account suffices to impress them.
Likewise for me a bunch of muscleboys
Suffices to create respect, *kapish?*
Respect from certain circles like Capone.
But little people are so difficult.
They're lousy snobs, the lot of them. Talk like
An Englishman, they think you're Jesus Christ.
    GIVOLA.
You're not exactly to the manner born,
Arturo. Some people are so sensitive
To hoke.
    UI.
          Some are, self-evidently so.
But who the hell cares what professors think,
Or city-slickers, intellectuals.
What counts is what the little hick imagines
Bosses act like. Basta now.
    GIVOLA.
                      But all the same
Why do you have to play the big shot, Chief?

Why don't you rather pick the father-image,
The ever-smiling popsy-wopsy type?

UI.

I've got old Dogsborough for that.

GIVOLA.

How long?
It seems to me the old man's slipping fast.
He looks a little shop-soiled nowadays.
Some people still consider him a plus,
A valuable piece of antique, but
They don't like to exhibit him so freely.
Perhaps they realize he's not authentic.
He does remind me of our fam'ly Bible,
Which Father wouldn't dare to look upon,
Not since the day when in the company
Of friends, he turned the yellow mellow pages,
As piously as ever, to discover
Squashed between Genesis and Exodus
The desiccated body of a louse.
Of course the old man's good enough to serve
As frontman for the Cauliflower Trust,
But . . .

UI.

I decide who's good enough for what.

GIVOLA.

I've nothing against Dogsborough as such.
He could be useful to us for a while.
Not even City Hall would drop him, yet.
The crash would be too loud.

UI. (*To the* ACTOR.)

How about sitting?

THE ACTOR. Sitting? Ah, sitting is about the hardest of
them all, Mr. Ui. There are actors who can walk. There
are actors who can stand. But where are the actors who
can sit? Take that armchair, Mr. Ui. Don't lean back.
Put your hands on your thighs, parallel to the stomach,
elbows away from the body. How long can you sit that
way, Mr. Ui?

UI.
As long as I want to.
    THE ACTOR.
Then all is well, Mr. Ui.
    GIVOLA.
Old Dogsborough won't live forever, Chief.
Have you considered his successor yet?
Giri the Joker is my candidate.
He's got a certain mass appeal, although
We've got no masses to appeal to yet.
He plays the clown and gives a belly-laugh
So loud the plaster falls from off the ceiling.
A very useful gift though now and then
He may abuse it, as for instance when
You tell the tale—it always breaks him up!—
How you, the simple son of Brooklyn, which
You really are, came west with seven buddies—
    UI.
He laughs about that?
    GIVOLA.
                                You should hear him, Chief.
He laughs so loud he makes the plaster peel.
Don't tell him, though, I told you, otherwise
He'll scream again that I am green with envy.
I wish, though, you could make him kick the habit
—'Tis most disgusting!—of collecting hats . . .
    UI.
What kinda hats?
    GIVOLA.
                            Of people whom he shot.
He promenades in public, wearing them.
    UI.
I will not muzzle my most loyal watchdog!
I do prefer to close my eyes to some
Small human weakness in my best assistants.
    (*To the* ACTOR.)
Now let's get down to speaking. Make a speech.
    THE ACTOR. Shakespeare of course. Nothing less will

do. Caesar, perhaps. The antique hero. (*Pulls a small book out of his pocket.*) How would you feel about Antony's speech? Over Caesar's coffin? Against Brutus. Chief of the Assassins. Model of popular oration. Played Antony in Zenith in 1908. They loved me in Zenith. Exactly what you need, Mr. Ui. (*He strikes a pose and starts reciting Antony's oration, line by line.*)
Friends, Romans, countrymen, lend me your ears!
(Ui *joins him, reading from the book, corrected occasionally by the* Actor, *but keeping his rough-and-tough tone.*)
I come to bury Caesar, not to praise him.
The evil that men do lives after them;
The good is oft interréd with their bones;
So let it be with Caesar. The noble Brutus
Hath told you Caesar was ambitious:
If it were so, it was a grievous fault:
And grievously hath Caesar answer'd it.
Here, under leave of Brutus and the rest,—
For Brutus is an honourable man;
So are they all, all honourable men,—
Come I to speak in Caesar's funeral.
He was my friend, faithful and just to me:
But Brutus says he was ambitious;
And Brutus is an honourable man.
He hath brought many captives home to Rome,
Whose ransoms did the general coffers fill:
Did this in Caesar seem ambitious?
When that the poor have cried, Caesar hath wept
Ambition should be made of sterner stuff:
Yet Brutus says he was ambitious:
And Brutus is an honourable man.
You all did see that on the Lupercal
I thrice presented him with a kingly crown,
Which he did thrice refuse: was this ambition?
Yet Brutus says he was ambitious;
And, sure, he is an honourable man.
I speak not to disprove what Brutus spoke,

But here I am to speak what I do know.
You all did love him once,—not without cause:
What cause withholds you then, to mourn for him?

(SLOW FADEOUT.)

*(A sign appears: HERR HITLER COACHED BY
PROVINCIAL ACTOR. LESSONS FROM HERR
BASIL IN ELOCUTION AND DEPORTMENT.)*

SCENE EIGHT

Offices of the Cauliflower Trust. UI, ROMA, GIVOLA, GIRI
and BODYGUARDS. UI *is haranguing a group of small-
time* GROCERS *from a platform. Next to him sits old*
DOGSBOROUGH, *looking ill. In the background,*
CLARK.

UI. (*Bellowing.*)
Murder! Butchery! Blackmail! Robbery! Fraud!
Guns chattering in public places. Men
Going about their peaceful occupations,
Solid citizens entering City Hall
To testify, mowed down by guns in daylight.
What are the City Dads doing about it?
Nothing. These so-called honorable men—
Their honor should be made of sterner stuff!—
Are busy spinning shady business plans
And shafting honest people in the back
Instead of giving them protection.
    GIVOLA.

                       Hear! Hear!
    UI.
But truth will come to light, fraud can't be hid too long!
To put it bluntly: Chaos reigns supreme
If everybody does as he damn pleases,

Prompted by egoism, which is a grievous fault,
Then everybody turns on everybody
Else, and chaos reigns supreme. Suppose I mind
My little store in peace or drive a truck
And hoodlums pump my tires full of holes,
Or trample through my store with "Stick 'em up!"
It is the end of law and order, yeh!
If on the other hand I understand
That man is not a man but just a dog,
And dog eats dog, I do something about it.
I stop my lousy fellow-human-being
From busting in whene'er the spirit moves him
And yelling, "Hey, reach for the sky or else!"
These hands have not been made to reach for heaven
But honest labor such as bottling pickles
Or cutting pizza. That's the way it goes.
Men will not yield their guns without coercion,
Only because it's nice to live in peace,
Or maybe they'll be praised by Nervous Nellies
In City Hall. You gotta shoot before
Somebody shoots you. That is logical.
Well, what to do, you must be wondering.
So listen to me careful. First things first.
The way you're acting just ain't good enough,
Hoping that all will turn out hunky-dory,
Grinding your lazy bums behind the counter
And fainting every time you see a thug.
You're disunited, splintered, and without
Some Big White Chief to give you firm protection.
So first comes unity. Then sacrifice.
I hear you say, "Why should we sacrifice?
Why dish out ten percent from off the top,
Or maybe twenty? Thank you very much.
There goes our little profit which we love.
Now if you did it free, that would be nice."
But grocers dear, nothing is free in life,
Except for mother-love. No other love!
There is a price-tag on security,

Such are the laws of life. They'll never change.
Thus I decided—with some other men—
And here they stand—and others stand outside—
To give you firm protection, come what may.

(GIVOLA *and* ROMA *cheer and applaud.*)

GIVOLA.
And now to show you that we're businesslike
And most professional, here's Mr. Clark.
You know him well. The Cauliflower King.
    (ROMA *brings* CLARK *forward. Some* GROCERS *applaud.*)
Welcome to this here meeting, Mr. Clark.
That you approve of Mr. Ui's plan
Does him—and you—much honor. Thank you, sir.
    CLARK.
Friends, countrymen, and fellow-grocers all!
We of the Trust have noted with alarm
How hard it is for you to make a buck.
We are familiar with your complaints.
"The stuff is too expensive!" Right you are!
But why is it expensive, friends? Because
Our drivers, packers, even shipping clerks,
Whipped up by agitators—foreign-born
No doubt!—are clamoring for higher wages.
But Mr. Ui and his gallant band
Of men would like to tidy up the mess.
    FIRST GROCER.
Sir, if you cut their wages even more,
Who's gonna come and buy our groceries?
    UI.
Your question is quite justified, my friend.
And let me answer you. Like it or not,
The workingman is here to stay. Yes, sir,
If only as a customer.
    GIVOLA.
                    Hear, hear.

UI.

I've always emphasized that honest work
Is not a badge of infamy. In fact,
It makes for profit and prosperity,
Which is why it's so very useful, right?

GIVOLA.

Right.

UI.

Yes, even I, the simple son of Brooklyn,
Did work my way through college as a youth,
By painting houses and et cetera.
The working stiff has all my sympathy,
So long he stays an individual.
But if the wise guy starts to organize
And sticks his goddamm nose into affairs
He doesn't understand, like lower wages,
Or higher profits and et cetera,
Then I must tell him: "Just a minute, brother!
Now that's enough. You are a workingman,
Which means you work. But if you stop to work
And take a walk along the picket-line,
Then you will cease to be a workingman,
And you'll become, and I'm a-quoting now,
The slander of your mother's heavy womb,
Subversive sonsabitches, all of you,
And basta, I must stop you dead.

(CLARK *applauds*.)

GIVOLA.

And now
To demonstrate our good faith, gentlemen,
It is my privilege to introduce
That marble-constant man, if I may say so,
The very model of unblushing honor.
Give him a hand, boys.

UI.

Mr. Dogsborough—

(*The* GROCERS *applaud a little louder.*)
Providence unites us in this hour.
I'd like to say how deeply I'm obliged.
I won't forget how you the Watchdog of
The Waterfront has picked this younger man,
This simple son of Brooklyn for a friend.
    (*Takes* DOGSBOROUGH's *flabby hand and starts pump-
ing it.*)
    GIVOLA. (*Half aloud.*)
A shattering moment! Father and son!
    GIRI.
Okay, you guys, you heard the Chief. He spoke
Straight from the shoulder and the heart. Come awn!
If you got any questions, fire away!
And don't be scared, nobody's gonna eat you.
Not if you toe the line. So here's the score:
Fruitless palaver ain't my cup of tea,
So let's have no more bullshitting around.
With Ifs and Buts and "Let me ask the wife!"
But if you got constructive-type ideas,
Go shoot the breeze. I'm all ears.

(*The* GROCERS *are silent.*)

    GIVOLA.
                         Don't be shy.
You know me and my little flower store.
I'm one of you . . .
    A BODYGUARD.
                  Ra-ra-ra-ra, Givola.
    GIVOLA.
What will it be, men, murder or protection?
Butchery, blackmail, force and violence . . .
    FIRST GROCER.
It's quiet in my neighborhood these days.
There's never been a fracas in my store.
    SECOND GROCER.
Neither in mine.

THIRD GROGER.
                Same here.
GIVOLA.
                              Remarkable.
SECOND GROCER.
We heard about some trouble in saloons
Like Mr. Ui told us. Glasses smashed
To bits, and liquor poured out on account
They wouldn't pay protection money. But
All is quiet in the groceries.
   ROMA.
                              And how
About Sheet's murder, eh? the death of Bowl?
   SECOND GROCER.
What's that to do with us or cauliflower?
   ROMA.
Nothing whatever. What's your name, my friend?
   SECOND GROCER.
Jim Crocket, sir.
   ROMA.
                Relax for just a minute.

(ROMA *goes up to* UI *who sits drained and lethargic after
   his tirade.* GIRI *and* GIVOLA *join them. A hasty,
   whispered conference.* GIRI *signals one of the* BODY-
   GUARDS. *They leave in a hurry.*)

   GIVOLA.
Distinguished friends, do lend me your attention:
I'm told some poor young lady just arrived,
Desirous to express her gratitude
To Mr. Ui.
   (*He goes to fetch a heavily rouged, jazzily dressed
   woman*—DOCKDAISY—*who has entered, holding a little
   girl by the hand. The three of them walk up to* UI.)
                Speak up, Mrs. Bowl.
   (*To the* GROCERS:)
She is, I hear, the widowed wife of Bowl,

Late treasurer to th' Cauliflower Trust,
Who, as you know, was slaughtered yesterday
By unknown murderers in City Hall
Where duty-bound he rushed to testify.

DOCKDAISY. Mr. Ui, stricken as I am with grief on account the dirty murder of my late-lamented husband, may he rest in peace, while he was discharging his duties as a citizen, I wish to express my heartfelt gratitude to you, especially for them beautiful flowers you sent me and my little girl of six who's been deprived of her father at such a tender age, too. (*To the* GROCERS.) Gentlemen, I'm only a poor widow but I gotta tell you this, I'd be in the streets tonight, except for Mr. Ui's generosity, and this I would always repeat under oath. My little girl of five and myself will never forget what you've done for us widows and orphans, Mr. Ui.

(UI *offers his hand to* DOCKDAISY, *tickles the little girl under the chin. Meanwhile* GIRI, *wearing Bowl's hat, is pushing his way through the crowd, followed by some gangsters disguised as truck-drivers, carrying kerosene cans. They leave.*)

UI.
My sympathies for your most grievous loss.
This ruthless and outrageous reign of terror
Has got to stop or else . . .

(*The* GROCERS *are about to leave.*)

GIVOLA.
                          Now just a minute.
The meeting isn't over yet, you know.
This poor bereaved woman needs support.
Dig in your pockets, pass the hat around
While Jimmy Greenwool here will sing a song
In memory of poor old Bernie Bowl.
Sit down, you guys! He is a baritone.

(*One of the* BODYGUARDS *sings a shmaltzy song. Eyes closed and chins propped up by hands, the* GANG-STER *sit listening with rapt attention.*)

GREENWOOL. (*Singing.*)
Our home stood by a weeping willow.
O Father, must you always roam?
There are three strange men looking through the window
Of what was once our dear old home.
I want my home again!
But a home is not the same as a house.
I want my home again!
But a house is not the same as a home.

(*Feeble applause by the* GROCERS, *interrupted by police whistles and sirens. A great window in the back is getting red.*)

ROMA.
Fire on the waterfront!
VOICES.
                              Where? What?
FIRST BODYGUARD. (*Entering.*)
                                        Is there
A grocer by the name of Crocket here?
SECOND GROCER.
Yes, why?
FIRST BODYGUARD.
              Your warehouse is on fire.

(CROCKET *rushes out. Some follow, others go to the window.*)

ROMA.
                              Stop!
Hold everything! Nobody leaves this room!
    (*To* FIRST BODYGUARD.)
It's arson, eh?

FIRST BODYGUARD.
        Yeh, sure, what else? They found
Some kerosene cans by the place.
    THIRD GROCER.
                    I saw
Some people walking out of here with cans.
    ROMA. (*In a rage.*)
What are you saying, man? That it was us?
    FIRST BODYGUARD. (*Digging a gun in a grocer's ribs.*)
Who did you say was carry'ng cans through here?
    ANOTHER BODYGUARD. (*To the other* GROCERS.)
You saw them cans? And you?
    GROCERS.
                 Not me. Not me.
    THIRD GROCER.
They looked like truck-drivers to me.
    ROMA.
                   You see!
The Chief was right! Them truck-drivers again!
It's all the fault of truck-drivers, my friend!
    GIVOLA. (*Talking fast.*)
The man who told us here a while ago
That all was hunkydory in the stores
Can see his warehouse going up in flames,
Turned into ash and rubble. Don't you see
The writing on the wall? Have you gone blind?
Unite, you guys, and now! The hour is late!
    UI. (*Wakes up from his apathy, roaring.*)
The city's gone too far. So first comes murder,
And arson next. Wake up, you men, I warn you!
Error is human, yeh, but so is terror.
Look outa window there! The heat is on!
For everyone! I do mean everyone!

(*A sign appears: FEBRUARY, 1033: REICHSTAG
BUILDING IN FLAMES. FRAMEUP TO
CRUSH OPPOSITION. HITLER STARTS
REIGN OF TERROR. "THE NIGHT OF THE
LONG KNIVES."*)

SCENE NINE

A street. A WOMAN, *streaming with blood, tumbles out of a shut-up truck.*

THE WOMAN.
Help! You! Don't run away! You gotta be
My witness! My husband in the truck is dead.
My arm is shot to bits. And so's the truck!
I need a bandage, or I'll bleed to death.
They're killing us like squashing flies on windows!
Help us! Oh God, why don't somebody help?
Is everybody gone? You murderers!
But I know who he is. He is that Ui!
    (*Raging.*)
You scum, you monster, oh, you crock of shit!
No, even shit would shudder seeing you
And, if you touched it, cry out, Let me wash!
Whoever touches Ui is defiled!
You louse of all the lice! And everyone
Will let him get away with it! You there,
They're hacking us to bloody pieces! Help!
It's Ui, Ui, Ui, and the rest!
    (*Machine-gun chattering nearby. She collapses.*)
Where are you, people? Help! Will no one stop the pest?

SCENE TEN

The Warehouse Fire Trial. PRESS, JUDGE, PROSECUTION,
DEFENSE, YOUNG DOGSBOROUGH, GIRI, GIVOLA,
DOCKDAISY, COURT PHYSICIAN, BODYGUARDS,
GROCERS, *and the accused* FISH.

A

(MANUELE GIRI *stands in front of the witness chair, wagging a finger at the accused* FISH *who sits in complete apathy.*)

GIRI. (*Screaming.*)
There is the man whose most atrocious hand
Had set the place on fire! Yes, he pressed
The kerosene can to his breast, when I
Arrested him. Stand up when I address you!

(FISH *is yanked out of his chair by ushers. He stands*
swaying.)

JUDGE. Accused Fish, pull yourself together. You're in
a court of justice. You're being accused of arson. Remember, your life is at stake. Now think.
FISH. (*Babbling.*) Ablah-blah-blah.
JUDGE. Where did you get the kerosene cans?
FISH. Ablah-blah.

(At the JUDGE'S *signal, the* COURT PHYSICIAN, *a sinister*
fop, leans over FISH *and exchanges glances with*
GIRI.)

COURT PHYSICIAN. He simulates, Your Honor.
DEFENSE COUNSEL. The defense requests that the
Court consult other medical experts.
JUDGE. (*Smiling.*) Overruled.
DEFENSE COUNSEL. Mr. Giri, how come you happened
to be on the scene of the fire which reduced Mr. Crocket's
warehouse and 22 other buildings to ashes?
GIRI. I was taking a digestive stroll.

(Some of the BODYGUARDS *laugh.* GIRI *joins in the*
laughter.)

DEFENSE COUNSEL. Mr. Giri, are you aware of the
fact that the defendant is an unemployed laborer who
arrived in Chicago on foot the day before the fire and
that he had never been in this town before?
GIRI. Wha'? When?
DEFENSE COUNSEL. Is the license number of your car
XXXXXX?

GIRI. That's right.

DEFENSE COUNSEL. Isn't it a fact that four hours before the outbreak of the fire your car was parked on 87th Street outside Dogsborough's saloon from where the defendant Fish was carried out in an unconscious condition?

GIRI. How should I know? I spent the day picnicking in Cicero where I met 52 people willing to swear they saw me.

(*The* BODYGUARDS *laugh.*)

DEFENSE COUNSEL. Didn't you just say you were taking a digestive stroll on the Chicago waterfront?

GIRI. You got any objections if I dine in one town and digest in another?

(*Big sustained laughter. The* JUDGE *laughs too. BLACK-OUT. An organ plays Chopin's Funeral March in jazz rhythm.*)

B

(*When the LIGHTS GO UP, the grocer* CROCKET *is in the witness chair.*)

DEFENSE COUNSEL. You ever had any conflict with the defendant, Mr. Crocket?

CROCKET. No.

DEFENSE COUNSEL. Can you think of any reason why he should burn your place down?

CROCKET. No.

DEFENSE COUNSEL. In fact, have you ever set eyes on him?

CROCKET. Never.

DEFENSE COUNSEL. How about Mr. Giri? Have you seen him before?

CROCKET. Yes, sir.

DEFENSE COUNSEL. Where?

CROCKET. At the offices of the Cauliflower Trust, the day my warehouse burned down.

DEFENSE COUNSEL. Before the outbreak of the fire?

CROCKET. Yes, immediately before.

DEFENSE COUNSEL. What was he doing?

CROCKET. Walking out with four people carrying kerosene cans.

(Tumult among the REPORTERS *and the* BODYGUARDS.*)*

JUDGE. Order in the press box! Order!

DEFENSE COUNSEL. Where was your warehouse located, Mr. Crocket?

CROCKET. Same block as the shipping line which used to belong to Mr. Sheet. Matter of fact, there's an alleyway connecting the two properties.

DEFENSE COUNSEL. Mr. Crocket, are you familiar with the fact that Mr. Giri is the superintendent of the shipping line and lives on the premises?

CROCKET. Yes, sir.

DEFENSE COUNSEL. D'you think he has access to the aforementioned alleyway?

CROCKET. He sure does.

(Pandemonium. The BODYGUARDS *boo and assume threatening attitudes toward the* DEFENSE COUNSEL, CROCKET *and the* PRESS. YOUNG DOGSBOROUGH *hurries up to the* JUDGE *and whispers in his ear.)*

JUDGE. Order! Owing to the defendant's indisposition, the Court is adjourned.

(BLACKOUT. The organ plays Chopin's Funeral March in jazz rhythm.)

C

(When the LIGHTS GO UP, CROCKET *is in the witness*

chair again, a broken man with a cane, his head and his eyes covered with a bandage.)

PROSECUTOR. How is your eyesight, Mr. Crocket?

CROCKET. (*With difficulty.*) Not very good.

PROSECUTOR. Would you say you're capable of recognizing a person instantly and without a doubt?

CROCKET. No.

PROSECUTOR. Do you, for instance, recognize that gentleman? (*Points at* GIRI.)

CROCKET. No.

PROSECUTOR. You couldn't say if you ever saw him, could you?

CROCKET. No.

PROSECUTOR. A final question, a very important question, Mr. Crocket. Think hard before you answer. Was your warehouse adjacent to the late Mr. Sheet's shipping line?

CROCKET. No.

PROSECUTOR. That's all.

(*BLACKOUT. The organ plays again.*)

D

(*When the LIGHTS GO UP,* DOCKDAISY *is in the witness chair.*)

DOCKDAISY. (*In a mechanical tone.*) I recognize the accused very easy on account the guilty expression on his face, and because he is five foot seven. Also, I heard from my sister-in-law that he was seen hanging around City Hall the day my husband was shot entering City Hall. He had an automatic pistol, model Webster, under his armpit and was making a suspicious impression.

(*BLACKOUT. The organ plays again.*)

E

(*When the LIGHTS GO UP*, GIUSEPPE GIVOLA *is in the witness chair. Nearby, the bodyguard* JAMES GREEN-WOOL.)

PROSECUTOR. We've heard testimony to the effect that before the outbreak of the fire some people were supposed to have left the offices of the Cauliflower Trust, carrying kerosene cans. Have you anything to say about these allegations?

GIVOLA. They could only be referring to Mr. Greenwool.

PROSECUTOR. Is Mr. Greenwool an employee of yours, Mr. Givola?

GIVOLA. Yes, sir.

PROSECUTOR. What is your occupation, Mr. Givola?

GIVOLA. I'm a florist.

PROSECUTOR. Is there an excessive amount of kerosene used in your line of business?

GIVOLA. (*Seriously.*) No, sir. Only for the extermination of plant lice, sir.

PROSECUTOR. What was Mr. Greenwool doing at the offices of the Cauliflower Trust?

GIVOLA. He was giving a song-recital.

PROSECUTOR. Could he have been carrying kerosene cans at the same time?

GIVOLA. No, sir.

PROSECUTOR. Could he have gone out to set Mr. Crocket's warehouse on fire?

GIVOLA. Singing?

PROSECUTOR. Answer the question directly.

GIVOLA. Absolutely impossible, sir.

PROSECUTOR. What makes you so sure, Mr. Givola?

GIVOLA. It is uncharacteristic of Mr. Greenwool to engage in inflammatory activities. He is a baritone.

PROSECUTOR. May it please the Court to permit the witness Greenwool to sing the beautiful song he sang at the offices of the Cauliflower Trust while the warehouse was being set on fire?

JUDGE. Singing irrelevant. Overruled.

GIVOLA.

I protest! (*Rises.*) This is discrimination!
These true-blue youngsters may occasionally
Go bang-bang-bang in juvenile excess,
Playful, not culpable, like kids on Halloween.
You treat them, sir, as shady customers.
Outrageous prejudice, and I protest!

(*Laughter. BLACKOUT. The organ plays again.*)

F

(*When the LIGHTS GO UP AGAIN, the courtroom shows signs of utter exhaustion.*)

JUDGE. According to rumors published in the press, the Bench is supposed, to be subject to pressure from certain quarters. The Bench wishes to state that no pressure has been brought upon it from any quarters whatsoever, and that'll do fine for a statement.

PROSECUTOR. Your Honor! In view of the fact that the accused Fish stubbornly persists in simulating schizophrenia, the prosecution holds that it is pointless to continue his cross-examination. We submit therefore . . .

DEFENSE COUNSEL. Your Honor! The defendant is coming to . . .

FISH. (*Seems to wake up.*) Wa . . . ter!

DEFENSE COUNSEL. Water! Your Honor, I call as my next witness the defendant Fish.

(*Uproar in court.*)

PROSECUTOR. I object, Your Honor! The accused is not in full possession of his mental faculties. The whole thing is a maneuver by the defense—cheap sensationalism!—to influence public opinion!

FISH. Wa . . . ter! (*Stands up with the help of the* DEFENSE COUNSEL.)

DEFENSE COUNSEL. Can you answer my questions, Fish?

FISH. Ye . . . eh.

DEFENSE COUNSEL. Fish, tell the Court in your own words: Did you on February 28th set fire to a vegetable warehouse in the dock district? Answer Yes or No.

FISH. No . . . na . . . no.

DEFENSE COUNSEL. When did you arrive in Chicago?

FISH. Water!

DEFENSE COUNSEL. Water!

(*Disorder in court.* YOUNG DOGSBOROUGH *has stepped up to the bench and is whispering to the* JUDGE.)

GIRI. (*Rises massively, bellowing.*) Machinations! Lies! Lies!

DEFENSE COUNSEL. Have you seen that man before? (*Points at* GIRI.)

FISH. Yes. Water!

DEFENSE COUNSEL. Where? Was it in Dogsborough's saloon on the waterfront?

FISH. (*In a low voice.*) Yeh.

(*Great tumult. The* BODYGUARDS *draw their guns and boo. The* COURT PHYSICIAN *comes running in with a glass and pours its contents down* FISH'S *throat before* DEFENSE COUNSEL *could stop him.*)

DEFENSE COUNSEL. I object! I demand this glass be examined!

JUDGE. (*Exchanging glances with the* PROSECUTOR.) Overruled!

DOCKDAISY. (*Screaming at* FISH.) Murderer!

DEFENSE COUNSEL.
Your Honor!
They can't stop up the mouth of truth with dirt,

So they shut her up with legal niceties,
Turning Your Honor's honor into shame.
They dig their rods into the ribs of justice,
Yelling "Hands up!" to her. Within a month
The town's grown old from fighting, with a groan,
A bloody brood that grew up into monsters.
We watched the slaughter of legality;
Now must we watch her violated too?
Her knees spread open as she yields to rape?
I beg Your Honor stop this rot!

PROSECUTOR.
                                                                Protest!

GIRI.
You dog! You dirty liar! Poison-mixer!
You jury-fixer, paid by Moscow Gold!
Step right outside, so I can tear your balls off!

DEFENSE COUNSEL.
Everybody knows about this man . . .

GIRI.
                                                              Shut up!
(*To the* JUDGE *who tries to interrupt.*)
                                                            You too!

You wanna stay alive? Then shut up too!

(*He stops, out of breath, giving the* JUDGE *a chance to
    address the Court.*)

JUDGE. Order, please! Counsel is fined five dollars for
contempt of court. The Bench is in full sympathy with
Mr. Giri's indignation. He's been sorely provoked. (*To*
DEFENSE COUNSEL.) Continue.

DEFENSE COUNSEL. Fish! Did anyone slip you a
Mickey Finn in Dogsborough's saloon?

FISH. (*His head droops flabbily.*) Ablah-blah-blah-
blah.

DEFENSE COUNSEL. Fish! Fish! Fish! Fish!

GIRI. (*Roaring.*)
                                    Call him till Doomsday come!

He's stalled just like a flivver in the snow!
I'll show you, man, who's boss of this here show!

(*Tumult. The organ plays again.*)

G

(*When the LIGHTS GO UP for the last time, the* JUDGE
*stands reading the sentence in a flat voice. The ac-
cused* FISH *is as white as chalk.*)

JUDGE. Charles Fish, the Court finds you guilty of
arson and sentences you to fifteen years imprisonment.

(*A sign appears: REICHSTAG FIRE TRIAL ENDS
IN UPROAR. GOERING LOSES TEMPER IN
COURT. DOPED LABORER SENTENCED TO
DEATH. MOCKERY OF JUSTICE.*)

SCENE ELEVEN

GIVOLA. (*Sings the "Song of the Whitewash."*)
Is there something foul and oozing from the plaster?
Does the dry rot drizzle through the wood?
Will the sewer spring a new disaster?
Then the situation isn't good.
But all we need is whitewash, fresh new coats of white-
     wash,
'Cause the pigsty's giving in to stress.
Give us whitewash, please! We'll do a bright wash!
Whistling while we work, to cover up the mess!
There's something new and nasty, peeling
Right across the kitchen ceiling!
And that's no good. (Not very good.)
Look, another crack, dear,
In the front and back, dear!
Ah, the system don't work like it should!

Do I hear a rumbling?
It's the roof that's crumbling!
That's no good (not very good).
So we need more whitewash, lots and lots of whitewash,
'Cause the pigsty's just about to quit!
Give us whitewash, please! We'll do a bright wash!
Whistling while we work, to cover up the shit!

SCENE TWELVE

Dogsborough's Country House. Dawn. DOGSBOROUGH *is*
writing his testament and confession.

DOGSBOROUGH.
Thus I, the honorable Dogsborough,
Past eighty winters spent in probity,
Permitted all this horror to be planned
And perpetrated by that bloody gang.
I hear that those who know me from before
Insist I did not know, for had I known
I'd not have tolerated all these crimes.
That's what they say. But I know everything.
O world! I know who burnt down Crocket's place.
I know who doped and kidnapped wretched Fish,
That Roma rubbed out Sheet most bloodily,
(A ticket in his pants for Santa Fé),
That Manuele Giri murdered Bowl
That rainy morning outside City Hall,
(He knew too much of honest Dogsborough!)
I know who beat good Crocket to a pulp;
I even saw him wearing Crocket's hat!
I know Givola mowed down seven more.
Please find a list of names enclosed. And last,
I know what Ui's done. He planned it all,
Beginning with the death of Sheet and Bowl
And all the way to open terrorism.
I knew it all and yet I let it pass,

I, Dogsborough, his honor turned to dust,
Seduced by greed, afraid to lose your trust.

SCENE THIRTEEN

Ui's suite at the Mammoth Hotel. UI *lies sprawling in
a deep armchair, staring into nothing.* GIVOLA *is
writing. Two* BODYGUARDS *look over his shoulders,
grinning.*

GIVOLA.
"Thus I, the honorable Dogsborough,
Leave my saloon to hard-working Givola,
My country house to brave though fiery Giri.
To upright Roma I bequeath my son.
For patronage, let merit be your guide:
Giri for Judge and Roma for Police Chief,
Relief and Welfare go to dear Givola.
As for my job, I heartily commend
Arturo Ui. Let him take my place.
He's worthy of the task, believe you me.
Yours Dogsborough." That ought to do the trick.
I hope the old man croaks and pretty soon.
He's had a stroke and now the city waits,
Rarin' to whitewash corpse and reputation;
They hope to dump the old man with decorum
Into some disinfected grave. He'll need
A tombstone with a fancy epitaph.
The raven too lives off his reputation,
The legendary raven that was white
And seen by someone sometime long ago.
The old man is the city's rare white raven.
They must be raving mad. Oh, by the way:
Your fav'rite boy, Emanuele Giri,
Spends too much time with Dogsborough. I think,
It's wrong.
    UI. (*Irritably.*)
            What's this with Giri?

GIVOLA.

'Morning, Chief.

I said he sees too much of Dogsborough.

UI.

I do not trust the guy.

(*Enter* GIRI *wearing Crocket's hat.*)

GIVOLA.

Neither do I.

Hi, Giri dear. How is the old man's stroke?

GIRI.

He still refuses to consult our doctor.

GIVOLA.

You mean the one who "cured" Defendant Fish?

GIRI.

I wouldn't let him see nobody else.

The old man is a blabbermouth, you know.

UI.

There may be other blabberers around.

GIRI.

Whaddayamean?

(*To* GIVOLA.)

You skunk, you made a stink

Again?

GIVOLA. (*Anxiously.*)

Here, Giri. Read the testament.

GIRI. (*Tears it out of his hand.*)

Roma Police Chief? Are you off your nut?

GIVOLA.

He wants the job, but I'm against it, too.

I wouldn't trust him with directing traffic.

(*Enter* ROMA *attended by* BODYGUARDS.)

Hello, Ernesto! There's the testament.

ROMA. (*Tears it out of* GIRI's *hand.*)

So Giri will be judge! Where is the real McCoy?

GIRI.

The old man has it still, and I suspect

He wants to make it public, but relax.
I stopped the son five times from smuggling out
The document.
>
> ROMA.
>
>   So hand it over, boy.

GIRI.

What d'you mean? I haven't got it, Ernie.

ROMA.

You've got it, creep. I know what you are up to.
(They face each other furiously.)
Sheet's murder must be mentioned in the will.
I wouldn't like to have it publicized.

GIRI.

Bowl's murder may be mentioned, too, you dope.
I wouldn't like to hit the headlines, either.
You gotta trust me, Ernie.

ROMA.

                    Hell I will.
You're rats, the both of you, but I'm a man.
I know you, Giri, and you, too, Givola.
You'd sell me to the stockyards for the glue.
I don't even believe your clubfoot's real.
You come here every time I turn my back.
What are they hissing in your ear, Arturo?
Don't go too far, you two. If I'm provoked
Again, I'll rub you out like bloody stains.

GIRI.

Don't talk to me as if I was a gangster!

ROMA.

What's wrong with be'ng a gangster, eh, you tell me?
(To his BODYGUARDS.*)*
You heard him, boys? It's you he's sneering at,
The hoity-toity, fancy-shmancy Giri,
Who dines and wines the cauliflower gents.
His silk shirt comes from Clark's own haberdasher.
He lets you do the dirty work.
(To UI.*)*

And you
Allow him to insult the boys.
   UI. (*As if waking up.*)
                     I, what?
   GIRI.
You let him blast the trucks of Mulberry,
And Mulberry is in the Trust, you know.
   UI. (*To* ROMA.)
You didn't shoot his trucks up, did you now?
   ROMA.
That was a slight case of misunderstanding
Which personally I did not authorize.
Some of the boys can't understand, Arturo,
Why all them crummy stores should sweat and bleed
And not the ritzy trucking firms as well.
Goddammit, I can't understand it either.
   GIVOLA.
The Trust is in a rage!
   GIRI.
                Clark warned me, Chief.
Next time a truck's molested, they will act.
That's why we went to see old Dogsborough.
   UI. (*Ill-tempered.*)
It mustn't happen, not again, Ernesto.
   GIRI.
You'd better do something about it, Chief.
These boys are getting too big for their britches.
   GIVOLA.
The Trust is in a rage!
   ROMA. (*Pulls a gun; to* GIRI *and* GIVOLA.)
               Now that's enough!
Reach for the sky, you two!
   (*To the* BODYGUARDS.)
              You, too, you goons!
Don't try no tricks. Stand up against the wall!
   UI. (*Indifferently.*)
What's going on here? What's the fight about?
You make me very nervous, Ernieboy.

A truck's been shot up. So? That can be squared.
Look, life's a bowl of cherries now, Ernesto.
And things are going like a house on fire.
That fire was a smash. The stores are paying
Up. Fifteen percent for some protection.
Within a week we forced the waterfront
Down to her knees. No hand is raised against us.
And I have further, bigger plans. . . .
    GIRI. (*Quickly.*)

                                    Like what?
Your plans be screwed! Tell him to let me drop
My hands.
    ROMA.

             It's safer if he keeps them up.
    GIVOLA.
We'll make a fine impression standing here
When Mr. Clark arrives. . . .
    UI.

                          Ernesto, dear,
Put down that fucking gun or else . . .
    ROMA.

                            Not I.
Wake up, Arturo! Don't you see the game?
They play you for a sucker, Chief, they do!
They sell you down the river to these Clarks
And Dogsboroughs! "When Mr. Clark arrives . . ."
It makes me puke. What happened to the loot
That we was promised from the City Loan?
We haven't seen a goddamm cent of it.
And while the boys go busting into stores
Or drag their cans to start a conflagration,
They moan and groan, "What happened to Arturo?
He doesn't give a shit for us no more!
He plays the big shot now. Wake up, Arturo!
    GIRI.
Wake up is right. Go chuck it up what chokes you!
Tell us whose side you're on.

GIVOLA.

Make up your mind!

UI. (*Jumps up.*)

Is this a Luger, which I see before me?
What's this, a pistol pressed against my breast!?
Oh no, you bullyboys! Not so, my friends!
You can't achieve a thing with me that way!
Whoever threatens me must face the consequence!
A milder man than I you never met,
But threats I can't abide. Whoever does not
Trust me blindly, let him walk alone. There is
No bargaining with me. With me it's either-or.
With me you do your duty or you're out
And I decide what you deserve, because
Deserving follows serving, gentlemen!
What I demand is trust and trust again!
And double trust! O ye of little faith!
How do you think I did create this thing?
I had the faith, a most fanatic faith
In Fate, the Cause, the Thing et cetera.
It was my faith and nothing but my faith
By which I muscled into town and forced her
On her knees. By faith I cornered Dogsborough.
By faith I entered City Hall. My naked
Hands did nothing hold but faith unshakable.

ROMA.

And a gun.

UI.

No! Others also have a gun.
But what they don't possess is holy faith
That they're predestined to be leaders. Friends,
Countrymen and Brooklynites, lend me your faith!
I gotta have your faith, you gotta give me faith!
I want the best for you, and I know best
What's best for you, and what's the best way to
Achieve our victory. Should Dogsborough
Drop dead, it's me—it's I—who will decide

Who will be doing what to whom and why.
But rest assured: you shall be satisfied.

GIVOLA. (*Hands over heart.*)

Arturo!

ROMA.

Scram! Wait, I want you-know-what.

GIRI.

I haven't got it on me.

ROMA. (*Frisking him.*)

Here it is.

Dogsborough's testament. The joke is over,
Joker. This time the laugh's on me. Skiddoo!

(GIRI, GIVOLA *and* GIVOLA's *bodyguards start out
slowly, hands up in the air.*)

Go shake a leg, man, crippled as it is,
And take your clubfoot back to where you stole it!

GIVOLA.

But, Roma, dear . . .

GIRI.

I like your hat.

ROMA.

Get out!

(*To* UI *who sinks into brooding again.*)
Dogsborough's testament and true confession!
And all the while he piled up horse manure
About not having it, he had it on him.

(*Reading from the testament.*)
"I know what Ui's done. He planned it all,
Beginning with the death of Sheet and Bowl
And all the way to open terrorism."

UI.

Leave me alone.

ROMA.

If I did not possess
The faith you spoke about so beautifully,
I couldn't look you in the eye, Arturo.
We gotta act and right away. That Giri
Is planning double-cross.

UI.

> Forget about him.

I'm planning bigger, better plans, Ernesto.
To you, my oldest friend and trusted aide,
I'll now divulge these monumental plans.
They're far advanced.

ROMA. (*Beaming.*)

> Go on! I'm listening!

(*He sits next to* UI. *The* BODYGUARDS *stand waiting in the background.*)

UI.

Chicago's in the bag. But I want more.

ROMA.

More?

UI.

> It's not the only place with groceries.

ROMA.

You mean the saints go marching on? Where to?

UI.

The front door and the back door and the window.
Invited or debarr'd, most welcome or rebuffed,
We'll beg and bully, threaten and cajole,
With iron hugs and velvet violence.
Or in a word: same mixture as before.

ROMA.

It may be different in other towns.

UI.

We'll have a little formal dress rehearsal
In a little town. A try-out, so to speak,
To test the audience in other places.
Although I doubt they're different from here.

ROMA.

Where would you have our little dress rehearsal?

UI.

Cicero.

ROMA.

> But Dullfeet is in Cicero,

Crusading for the vegetable cause,
Screams Independence! for the local stores.
He fears their salad days be over soon.
His paper calls me names. Sheet's Murderer!
   Ui.
That ought to stop.
   Roma.
                It could.
   Ui.
                     It must.
   Roma.
                        It will.
Black print makes many men see red. Like me.
   Ui.
It must be stopped at once. Negotiations
By the Trust have just begun in Cicero.
We want to start by selling cauliflower
Nice and easy.
   Roma.
            Who's negotiating?
   Ui.
                  Clark.
   Roma.
So Mr. Big himself is in the act!
I wouldn't trust him with a pickle, Chief.
   Ui.
He's having trouble. On account of us.
They cry in Cicero: "They're everywhere!"
They say we are the shadows of the Trust.
They want their cauliflower but not us.
The little grocers shiver at our name.
Not only them. Fair Mrs. Dullfeet too,
Who owns the most important export-import
Wholesale vegetable outfit in the town.
She'd like to be a member of the Trust
But will not merge as long as we're around.
   Roma.
You mean the plan to conquer Cicero

Is not your own? The Trust has dreamt it up?
I see, Arturo! Now I see the light!
It's clear what game is played. . . .
    UI.

                            Where?

   ROMA.

                            In the Trust.

And in the country house of Dogsborough!
His testament was ordered by the Trust!
They want to annex little Cicero.
You block the way. They gotta dump you first!
You got them by the balls. You know the dirt.
They made you do their dirty work, but now
They'd like to drop you like a hot potato.
So here's the gimmick: Dogsborough confesses!
Beating his breast, he dresses up in sackcloth,
Crawls penitent from sickbed into limelight,
Surrounded by them cauliflower gents
Who deeply moved produce this testament
And read it to the press: How Dogsborough
Regrets his error, urgently demanding
Exterminate the rats who spread the plague
Which he—to err is human—helped to breed.
But that's enough! Let us revive the old
And venerable vegetable trade.
That is the plot, and they are all in it,
Giri who helped to write the testament,
Best pal to Clark who thinks we're two-bit punks;
Clark wants no shadow when he shakes the plums
Of Cicero. Givola, too, the dungfly,
Buzzing about you like you was a corpse.
And good old honorable Dogsborough
Who smears you in this sland'rous document.
They're all in it, they're all in it, Arturo!
You gotta liquidate them, Chief. Tonight!
Be stirring as the time, be fire with fire,
Threaten the threatener . . .

Uɪ.

You mean they're in cahoots?
They wouldn't let me visit Cicero . . .
I wondered why.

Roma.

Chief, let me clear the decks!
The boys and me will take a trip tonight,
To snatch old Dogsborough from out his bed.
We'll say we'll move him to the hospital
And drop him—bye-bye blackbird!—at the morgue!

Uɪ.

But Giri's there. . . .

Roma.

He likes the country air.
I'll take him for a ride around the lake.
(*They look at each other.*)
It's wash-up time.

Uɪ.

And how's about Givola?

Roma.

I'll see him on the way back in his store,
To order heavy wreaths for Dogsborough
And laughing Giri, too. I'll pay in kind.
(*Shows his gun.*)

Uɪ.

Ernesto, I am much obliged to you.
I see it now. It's an outrageous plot!
So Giri, Clark, Givola, Dogsborough
Wish to include me out of Cicero
By labelling me as a crook in public!
You gotta nip this libel in the bud
Most brutally, Ernesto. I rely
On you.

Roma.

You bet. But, Chief, you gotta come
To coach the boys before we make the move,
To sic 'em in the right direction. I'm
Not so good at making speeches.

Uɪ. (*Shakes his hand.*)

I'll be there.

ROMA.
I knew it, knew it all the time, Arturo!
The two of us together—you and me!

Uɪ.
What time?

ROMA.

Eleven sharp.

Uɪ.

Where?

ROMA.

The garage.

Uɪ.
I'll see you there most punctual on the hour.

ROMA. (*To the* BODYGUARDS.)
He is with us. What did I tell you, boys?
I feel a different man, Arturo,
We'll dare the world together once again!
Yeh, men! It's like the good old days again!

(*He exits quickly with his* BODYGUARDS. Uɪ *walks up and
down, rehearsing the speeech he will make to* ROMA's
men.)

Uɪ.
Friends!
Regretfully I must announce to you:
It's come to my attention recently:
Abominable treason's being planned
Behind my back or thereabouts, I'm told.
Men of my most immediate entourage,
Whom I have trusted, are reportedly
Hatching a rotten plot, running amuck
With greed and envy, treacherous by nature
And in cahoots with th' Cauliflower Gents
—That doesn't sound right. In cahoots with who?

I've got it! The police!—They sold me out
And plan to send me to my forcéd grave,
With 67 bullets in my gut.
No wonder that my patience is exhausted!
I order you that led by Ernie Roma,
Who has my confidence, you whip these thugs
From out the circle of my territories.

(*Enter suddenly* GIRI *with* CLARK *and* BETTY DULL-
FEET. UI *jumps with fright.*)

GIRI.
It's only us, Chief. You got company.
CLARK.
Meet Mrs. Dullfeet, here from Cicero.
Ui, the Trust would like you to consider
Her proposition very carefully.
UI. (*Darkly.*)
I'm listening.
CLARK.
                And come to some agreement.
UI.
Please proceed.
CLARK.
                Negotiations for a merger
Between Chicago's vegetable trade
And Cicero's have been suspended now.
Doubt raised its ugly head in Cicero
About the methods of your syndicate.
The Trust has managed to dispel these doubts
And Mrs. Dullfeet's come . . .
MRS. DULLFEET.
                            To clear the air;
Remove misunderstandings, Mr. Ui.
In Mr. Dullfeet's name I wish to stress
His recent press crusade was not addressed
To you.
UI.
        Who else?

CLARK.
                              I'll give it to you straight,
Ui. The so-called suicide of Sheet
Made everybody mad in Cicero.
The man had some distinction, after all.
He was the owner of a shipping line,
Whatever else he may have been. He was
Not just a nobody who bummed a ride,
Like certain bums we know. Another thing:
Good Mulberry's garages keep complaining:
Their trucks begin to look like cheese on wheels.
Two incidents involving you-know-who.
  MRS. DULLFEET.
Every child in Cicero can tell you:
The cauliflower of the Trust is smeared
With blood. They know who makes it bleed.
  UI.
                                        So what?
Outrageous gossip, if you ask me.
  MRS. DULLFEET.
                              Sir . . .
  UI.
They spit their malice in my face!
  MRS. DULLFEET.
                              Not yours!
No, no, it wasn't you I had in mind.
Since Mr. Clark has vouched for you, we are
Concerned with only Ernie Roma.
  UI. (*Rising.*)
                              Yeh?
  CLARK. (*Quickly.*)
Keep cool, Arturo!
  GIRI.
                  Take it easy, Chief!
  UI.
I will not listen! What d'you take me for?
Enough! Enough! Ernesto is my friend!
I will not be dictated to what kind

Of men I want to have about me, ma'm.
That is an insult I won't tolerate.
    MRS. DULLFEET.
Ignatius Dullfeet will continue fighting
Such men as Roma till his dying breath.
    CLARK. (*Coolly.*)
And rightly so. The Trust will back him up.
Ui, be sensible. You know damn well
That friendship doesn't mix with business. Well?
    UI. (*Equally cool.*)
There's nothing I can add to what I said.
    CLARK.
Dear Mrs. Dullfeet, I regret profoundly
The outcome of this conference.
    (*To* UI; *leaving.*)
                                    Unwise!

(UI *and* GIRI *are left alone. They don't look at each
    other.*)

    GIRI.
You like your troubles big?
    UI.
                    I'm not afraid.
    GIRI.
Okay, you're not afraid. You only picked a fight
With Dogsborough, the cops, the Press, the Trust
And everyone with muscle in this town.
Listen to reason, Chief, and call them back.
    UI.
I know my sacred duty as a friend.
    GIRI.
Duty be screwed.
    UI.
                    Remove yourself.
    GIRI.
                                    Not nice!
    UI.
I'll let you know, sir, when I need advice.

*(A sign appears: HINDENBURG'S DEATH IMMI-
NENT. BITTER STRUGGLES WITHIN NAZI
CAMP. HERR HITLER UNDER PRESSURE,
INFLUENTIAL CIRCLES DEMAND REMOVAL
OF S.A. CHIEF ERNST ROEHM.)*

SCENE FOURTEEN

*A garage. Night. Sound of rain. ERNESTO ROMA and
young INNA. In the background, some gunmen.*

INNA.
It's now struck one.
  ROMA.

               He must have been delayed.
  INNA.
Could be he can't make up his mind.
  ROMA.

                      Could be.
Arturo's so attached to all his men
That he would rather sacrifice himself,
Recoiling from the very thought of striking
Than crush these vermin, Giri and Givola.
And so he dawdles, wrestling with his soul.
Reluctantly he lingers in the night.
It may be two o'clock before he comes.
Or maybe three. But come what may he'll come.
I know him, Inna.
  INNA.

           Oh, these rainy nights!
They give me gooseflesh.
  ROMA.

              That's what I like, my boy.
"Of all the nights the blackest ones,
Of all the cars the quickest ones,
Of all the friends, the steady ones."

INNA.
                              How long
You've known Arturo?
    ROMA.
                          Eighteen years.
    INNA.
                              That's long.
    A GUNMAN.
The boys would like to drink a little something.
    ROMA.
They can't. Tonight I want them sober.

   (*The* BODYGUARDS *bring in* SHORTY.)

    SHORTY.
                                Boss,
It looks like dynamite. Two armored cars
Have left the precinct station, full of cops.
    ROMA.
The shutters down! It may be false alarm,
But better worry than be sorry, like
The Boy Scouts say.
   (*The steel shutters of the garage door slowly descend.*)
                   Is all clear in the alley?
    INNA. (*Nods.*)
Tobacco is remarkable. You light
A cigarette. You smoke. You look real tough
And deep inside you feel like jellyfish.
But then you act like you were really tough
And in the end, who knows, you're really tough.
    ROMA. (*Smiling.*)
Show me your hands.
    INNA. (*Obeys.*)
                   They're trembling, which is bad.
    ROMA.
What's bad about it? Let me take your hand.
I don't think much of bullyboys. They are
Insensitive. No one can hurt them, so

They don't know how to hurt. Not seriously.
Go tremble, boy. The compass trembles too
Before the needle settles down to rest.
Your hands are looking for the Pole, that's all
It is.

VOICE. (*Outside.*)
　　Police car cruising down the street.

ROMA. (*Sharply.*)
It stops?

VOICE.
　　　　It goes. No. Parks behind the church.

A GUNMAN. (*Entering.*)
Two cars around the corner, headlights dimmed.

ROMA.
They're gunning for Arturo, that's for sure.
O the bastards, Giri and Givola!
They sold him out. He'll walk into a trap.
We gotta cut him off.

A GUNMAN.
　　　　　　It's suicide.

ROMA.
Well, if it's suicide, this is the time
For suicide, man. Eighteen years of friendship!

INNA. (*In a high voice.*)
Raise the shutters! Got the choppers ready?

A GUNMAN.
Sure.

INNA.
　　Giddy-up!

(*The steel shutters rise slowly. The headlights of a car,
　　approaching. UI and GIVOLA enter quickly, followed
　　by BODYGUARDS.*)

ROMA.
　　　　Arturo!

INNER. (*In a low voice.*)
　　　　　　And Givola!

ROMA.
What's going on? We've sweated blood for you!
(*Laughs loud.*)
Gee, boss, are you all right?
   UI. (*Hoarsely.*)
                        Why shouldn't I
Be all right?
   INNA.
               We thought something'd gone wrong. Go
Shake him by the hand, Chief. He was about
To take us all the way to hell for you.

(UI *walks up to* ROMA, *offering his hand. Laughing,*
   ROMA *takes* UI's *hand which prevents him from*
   reaching for his Browning when GIVOLA *whips out*
   his gun and, firing from the hip, shoots ROMA.)

   UI.
Line them up against the wall.

(ROMA'S MEN, *flabbergasted, are driven into a corner.*
   GIVOLA *bends over* ROMA *who is lying on the floor.*)

   GIVOLA.
                    Still breathing.
   UI.
Finish him off.
   (*To those standing against the wall.*)
              Your infamous attempt on me,
Likewise the plan to murder Dogsborough
Has been unmasked. I've come to foil it at
Th' eleventh hour. It's useless to resist.
Fine flock of buzzards! Don't you make a move!
I'll teach you, bastards, what it means to try
To knife me in the back.
   GIVOLA. (*Bending over* ROMA.)
                   He's coming to.

UI.

I'll spend the night with Dogsborough.

(*Walks out quickly.*)

INNA.

You rats!

You dirty rats!

GIVOLA. (*Excitedly.*)

Go let 'em have it!

(*The MEN at the wall are mowed down by submachine guns.*)

ROMA. (*Coming to.*)

Hell!

Givola!

(*He turns around heavily, chalk-white in the face.*)

O, what happened there?

GIVOLA.

Not much.

Few traitors executed.

ROMA.

Oh, you dog!

What have you done to all my people?

(GIVOLA *is silent.*)

Christ!

What's with Arturo? Murder! Oh, I knew it!

I'm going blind. Where is he?

(*Crawls across the floor, looking for UI.*)

GIVOLA.

Gone.

ROMA. (*While he is dragged to the wall.*)

You dogs!

GIVOLA. (*Coolly.*)

You called me once a crooked cripple. Well,

Let's see, my friend, how straight you walk to hell.

(*Shoots ROMA.*)

(*A sign appears: JUNE 30, 1934: S.A. CHIEF ROEHM*

AND FRIENDS AMBUSHED WHILE WAITING FOR HITLER TO STAGE COUP AGAINST HINDENBURG AND GOERING. MASSACRE AT TAVERN.)

SCENE FIFTEEN

Givola's flower-store. Enter IGNATIUS DULLFEET, *no bigger than a boy, and* BETTY DULLFEET.

DULLFEET.
I don't like the idea.
     BETTY.
                              Why not, Ignatius?
Roma's gone.
     DULLFEET.
                    Murdered, you mean.
     BETTY.
                                        Whichever way
He may have gone, he's gone. And Clark has told me
That Ui's youthful revels are now ended.
—The best of us have gone through *Sturm und Drang*—
He's sown his wild oats, so to speak, and shown
His manner and his grammar much improved:
He hasn't murdered anyone for weeks.
But if you do persist attacking him,
You might revive his baser instincts yet,
And put yourself in jeopardy, Ignatius.
But if you keep your mouth shut, they'll be nice.
     DULLFEET.
I doubt if silence helps.
     BETTY.
                            It helps a little.
These people are not animals.

(GIRI *enters from the back of the store, wearing* ROMA'S *hat.*)

GIRI.
                              Hello!
The Chief will be delighted. He's in the back.
I must be off, unfortunately. And
On the double, too, before Givola
Sees me in this hat. I've pinched it from him.
    (*He laughs so loud that plaster falls from ceiling, and
    exits waving his hand.*)
DULLFEET.
It's bad enough to hear them growl, but worse
To hear them laugh.
    BETTY.
                        Don't speak so loud, Ignatius.
Not here.
    DULLFEET. (*Bitterly.*)
            And nowhere else.
    BETTY.
                                What can we do?
The word is out that Ui will inherit
The late-lamented Dogsborough's position.
What's worse, the grocers swing toward the Trust.
    DULLFEET.
Two of my printing presses smashed to bits.
Woman, I have a premonition . . .
    BETTY. (*In a low voice.*)
                                Ui!

    (*Enter* UI *and* GIVOLA, *hands stretched out.*)

    UI.
Dullfeet, welcome!
    DULLFEET.
                Sir, I'll be frank with you.
I did not want to come at all. . . .
    UI.
                                How come?
Courageous men are welcome everywhere.

GIVOLA.
And so are lovely ladies.
DULLFEET.

Mr. Ui,
I feel it is my duty to oppose you . . .
UI. (*Cutting in.*)
Misunderstandings! If you and I had known
Each other from the very start, I doubt
It would have come to this. I've always hoped
To settle everything that should be settled,
Must be settled, amicable.
DULLFEET.

Violence. . . .

UI.
No one abhors it more than I. Alas,
If men would only yield to reason, sir,
No violence was ever necessary.
DULLFEET.
My aim in life . . .
UI.

. . . Is quite the same as mine.
Business in bloom, that's what we want, correct?
To see the little groceries, whose lot
Is not exactly rosy nowadays,
Selling their groceries in peace, and seek
Protection when attacked.
DULLFEET. (*Firmly.*)

Let them be free to choose
Whether they want protection, Mr. Ui.
That is my most important . . .
UI.

I agree.
They *must* be free to choose or else. But once
They've chosen their protectors freely, sir,
They might as well give up a bit of freedom
To those they've chosen freely to protect
Their little freedoms—to ensure us all
That confidence reigns in the groceries

And other places where it's sorely needed.
I've always been a confidence—I mean—
I've always stressed the need for confidence.
   DULLFEET.
I'm glad to hear it straight from you, Ui.
But at the risk of stepping on your toe,
Do let me warn you, sir, that Cicero
Will never yield to force. . . .
   UI.
                     That's understandable!
Nobody yields to force unless he's forced to.
   DULLFEET.
Let me be blunt. If this new merger with the Trust
Will ever lead to all that bloody mess
Which keeps harassing old Chicago town,
I'll never let you get away with it.
   UI.
Why, Mr. Dullfeet! Bluntness calls for bluntness.
It's not impossible that in the past
An incident or maybe two occurred
That wouldn't pass the strictest moral test.
Such things do happen in a fight, my friend,
But not among friends. Dullfeet, all I ask:
Give me your confidence. Forget the past.
Consider me a friend who would not ever,
No, never ditch a friend. To be specific:
I would appreciate if you refrained
From printing all them horror-tales about me.
They aggravate my sensitivity.
   DULLFEET.
I would be happy to keep quiet, Ui,
If things were quiet, too.
   UI.
                     They will be quiet.
But if occasionally some episode occurs,
Because a man's a man, sir, not a saint,
I hope you won't be screaming bloody murder.
I couldn't guarantee that now and then

One of our drivers might not use a cussword,
Reflecting on your mother's chastity.
That's only human, after all. And if
By any chance a grocer buys a beer
To please a salesman—prompt delivery
Of cabbage on his mind—such harmless practices
Should not be misconstrued as bribery.

BETTY.
My husband's only human, Mr. Ui.

GIVOLA.
He's famous for that fact, madam. And now
That everything's been peacefully resolved
—A friend in need's a friend indeed, they say—
I'd like to show you 'round my little store.

UI.
Ignatius, after you.

(*They start inspecting* GIVOLA'S *flowers.* UI *leads* BETTY,
GIVOLA *leads* DULLFEET. *In the following scene they
keep popping in and out of the flower-arrangements.*
GIVOLA *and* DULLFEET *appear. MUSIC.*)

GIVOLA.
Dwarfed Japanese oaks. Don't you find them charming?
Blooming round a rock-pool.

DULLFEET.
                                    What's that in it, snarling?

GIVOLA.
Goldfish having dinner. Full of airs and graces.

DULLFEET.
Snapping after bread crumbs . . .

GIVOLA.
                                    As the human race is.

DULLFEET.
The man who's fond of flowers surely can't be vicious.

GIVOLA.
The big fish always wonders where the little fish is.

(*They disappear.* UI *and* BETTY *appear.*)

BETTY.

A strong man need not exercise his power.

UI.

I need my exercise.

BETTY.

                    Then say it with a flower.

Gentle persuasion can be heaps of fun.

UI.

Madam, the most persuasive thing's a gun.

BETTY.

I've come to move your heart, sir, and to prove . . .

UI.

Ladies, I'm told, are not supposed to move.

BETTY.

There's nothing like an honest give-and-take.

UI.

Especially for those who only take.

BETTY.

Oh, why d'you always show the iron fist?

UI.

Dear Mrs. Dullfeet, I'm a realist.

(They disappear. GIVOLA *and* DULLFEET *reappear.)*

DULLFEET.

Flowers, they say, are ignorant of sin.

GIVOLA.

That's why I picked the business I am in.

DULLFEET.

They lead such peaceful lives. Look at the daisy!

GIVOLA.

She's got no daily press to drive her crazy.

(They disappear. BETTY *and* UI *reappear.)*

BETTY.

I understand your habits are Spartanic.

UI.

Liquor, tobacco, sex: they make me panic.

BETTY.
I can't quite see you, sir, among the saints.
UI.
When tempted in the flesh, Arturo faints.
BETTY.
I make you feel . . . ?
UI.
                              Get thee behind me, Satan!
I disapprove of . . .
BETTY.
                    Say it!
UI.
                              Fornicating.

(*They disappear.* DULLFEET *and* GIVOLA *reappear.*)

DULLFEET.
It must be nice to spend your life 'mong flowers.
GIVOLA.
It could be nice. But there are other powers.

(*They disappear.* UI *and* BETTY *reappear.*)

BETTY.
What is your true opinion on religious questions
UI.
Some of my best friends, like myself, are Christians.
BETTY.
The Ten Commandments? Like "Thou shalt not kill"?
UI.
In business? Too demanding and impractical.
BETTY.
Sorry to plague you with a final question:
What are your views on. . . .
UI.
                    Say it!
BETTY.
                              The Depression.

UI.
I've always been a social-minded creature.
The poor get poorer, but that's human nature.

(*They disappear.* DULLFEET *and* GIVOLA *reappear.*)

DULLFEET.
Flowers do not mix well with criminals.
GIVOLA.
And how! At funerals! What funerals!
DULLFEET.
I quite forgot. Death is your daily bread.
GIVOLA.
Some of my nicest customers are dead.
DULLFEET.
Let's hope you find some other use for posies.
GIVOLA.
For those who know to take a hint *sub rosas.*
DULLFEET.
Threats do not pay, Givola. Nor does force.
GIVOLA.
Then someone else must pay.
DULLFEET.
                        We're mixing metaphors.
GIVOLA.
You look so pale.
DULLFEET.
            I find it hard to breathe.
GIVOLA.
Perhaps you are allergic to this wreath.

(*They disappear.* BETTY *and* UI *reappear.*)

BETTY.
I'm so relieved. We understand each other.
UI.
You're just as understanding as my mother.
BETTY.
Friendships maturing in trouble and strife . . .

UI.
Thank God for broads who know the facts of life.

(DULLFEET *and* GIVOLA *reappear*.)

DULLFEET.
Betty, let's go. I can't abide this place.
BETTY.
Farewells, at times, are very hard to face.
UI. (*To* DULLFEET.)
That you and I have come to an agreement—
A most propitious sign . . .
GIVOLA. (*Aside*.)
For his bereavement.
DULLFEET.
Remember, sir, I'll not forget my duty.
UI.
Neither will I.
GIVOLA. (*Offers a bouquet to* BETTY.)
Here. Beauties for a beauty.
DULLFEET and BETTY.
Farewell, Farewell, for we must needs be gone.
UI. (*Aside*.)
His eyes do show his days are almost gone.

(*A sign appears: AUSTRIA YIELDS TO NAZI CA-
JOLING, CHANCELLOR ENGELBERT DOLL-
FUSS CALLS OFF PRESS ATTACKS*.)

SCENE SIXTEEN

*The cemetery of Cicero. CHURCH BELLS. A cortège
is moving toward a mausoleum. Behind the coffin
walks* BETTY DULLFEET *in widow's weeds, followed
by* CLARK, UI, GIRI, GIVOLA. *The last three carry
enormous wreaths which they deposit in the mausoleum and return. The voice of the* PASTOR *is heard
from inside the mausoleum.*

PASTOR'S VOICE.
The mortal coils of Dullfeet come to rest.
Poor in reward yet rich in toil, his life
Is ended. Much toil expended in that life,
Not for the gain of him who spent it toiling,
And now is gone. We wish him happy landing.
At heaven's gate, to greet him when he enters
A flight of angels touch thy worn-out shoes
And sing thee to thy sleep with "Here's a man
Who bore the load of multitudes." And when
The City Council meets in grand assembly
And every man has had his say, there'll be
A little silence. They'll be wondering
When will Ignatius Dullfeet filibuster?
Indeed we are so used to hear him speak,
It seems the city's conscience has been silenced,
For he who's gone from us so prematurely,
He knew the straight and narrow path by heart,
Could walk it blindly, never lost his way.
His flesh was rather small, his spirit huge,
His voice as editor was clarion-clear,
Echoing far beyond the city's range.
Ignatius Dullfeet, rest in peace. Amen.
    GIVOLA.
No word how Dullfeet died. A tactful man.
    GIRI. (*Puts on* DULLFEET'S *hat.*)
A tactful man? A man with seven kids.

(CLARK *and* MULBERRY *come out of the mausoleum.*)

    CLARK.
Goddammit, are you standing guard to stop
The truth from being heard e'en at the coffin?
    GIVOLA.
Dear Clark, you're being very harsh. The ground
You stand on ought to make you kinder, sir.
Besides, the Chief is sad today. This is
No place for him to spend a quiet weekend.

MULBERRY.
You butchers! Dullfeet kept his word to you!
He kept his mouth shut about everything.
GIVOLA.
Silence is not enough. We need the guys
Who're ready to speak up for us, and loud.
MULBERRY.
What's there to speak about you guys, except
That you're a bunch of goons?
GIVOLA.
                                        He had to go.
That little man was like the pores through which
The fearful perspiration of the trade
Kept pouring out. It stank, that sweat of fear.
GIRI.
And how's about your cauliflower, boys?
D'you want it sold in Cicero or not?
CLARK.
Not by assassination.
GIRI.
                              So what else?
You'd like to have your steak and eat it, too,
But bawl us out for slaughtering the steer.
You howl for meat but when you see the axe,
You call the cook a bloody butcher. Oh,
I like that. No sirree! What we expect
Is gratitude and not abuse. Go home.
MULBERRY.
The day we met them was our blackest day.
CLARK.
You're telling me.

(*They leave gloomily.*)

GIRI. (*To* UI.)
                        This is a funeral.
Don't let them bastards spoil your fun.

GIVOLA.

Watch out.

Look where she comes.

(BETTY DULLFEET *enters from the mausoleum, supported by a* WOMAN. *ORGAN MUSIC from the mausoleum.*)

UI.

My sympathies, madam.

(*She walks past him without a word.*)

GIRI. (*Yelling.*)
Hey, you, stop!

(*She stops and turns around. She is as white as chalk.*)

UI.

I said: My sympathies, madam.
Dullfeet, God bless him, is no more, no more,
But Cauliflower's here to stay. You may
Not see it quite what with your vision blurred
By tears. But Dullfeet's most untimely fall
Must not make you forget that in the night
Killcrazy goons from craven ambush firing
Are busy blasting vegetable trucks
And their hell-governed hands pour kerosene
To make your precious vegetables rot.
But here we stand, my friends and I, to pledge
Protection. What d'you say?
    BETTY. (*Glancing heavenwards.*)

Ye Gods, d'you hear?
And Dullfeet not yet turned to dust!
    UI.

I, too,
Lament obsequiously his demise.
That man, struck down by ruthless hands, he was
My friend.

BETTY.

That's right. The hand that struck him down,
The selfsame hand that shook him by the hand,
Was yours.

UI.

Dame Gossip, there you go again!
I am provoked by sland'rous tongues again!
They pour their poison on my best intention
Which is, quite simply, "Love thy neighbor." Yeh!
This Let's-Misunderstand-Him Drive again,
This Wooing-Taken-For-Dragooning. Oh,
This lack of trust when I do trust them so!
They slap my hand whene'er I stretch it out—

BETTY.

To strangle anyone who's in your way.

UI.

No!

I'm being friendly and fanatically!
Why do you spit on me?

BETTY.

As friendly as a snake
Who sneaks up on a rabbit.

UI.

D'you hear that, boys?
That's how I'm treated. Yes, that's even how
This Mr. Dullfeet had miscalculated
My glowing friendship for an artful dodge,
My generosity for weakness. Too bad
For him. I sowed the seeds of friendliness
And reaped a crop of icy silence. Oh
Yeh, silence was the answer when I hoped
For happy partnership. And how I hoped to see
My stubborn, nay, humiliating pleas
For friendliness repaid by what? A bit
Of understanding, oh, one little sign
Of human warmth, but no, I hoped in vain,
And all I ever got was grim contempt.
And e'en that silence, oh, the famous silence,

Promised morosely with demurring faces,
They broke that promise on the first occasion.
Yes, ma'm, where is your celebrated silence?
You blow your horn in every which direction
To advertise your horror-tales about me.
I'm warning you. Don't go too far, my dear.
You can't rely on my proverbial patience.

BETTY.

I'm speechless.

UI.

Speechlessness is heartlessness.

BETTY.

D'you call it heart, the thing that makes you speak?

UI.

I speak the way I feel.

BETTY.

Can anybody
Feel the way you speak? Yes, I believe you can.
You murder from the bottom of your heart,
Your crimes are deeply felt as other people's
Charity. You trust in treason as we trust
In God. Steadfast you are in fickleness,
And incorruptible by any noble passions.
Sincere in lying, honest in deceiving,
Inspired by any beastly act, and most
Enthusiastic at the sight of blood.
Was there brutality? Your heart leaps at the news.
Is that a dirty deal? You are reduced to tears.
And every deed of kindness makes you moved
With hatred and revenge.

UI.

Mrs. Dullfeet:
It is my principle to listen calm
When my opponent wants to speak, although
He may be most abusive. Oh, I know,
I'm not exactly pop'lar with your friends.
They've never quite forgiven me my roots.
I'm after all the simple son of Brooklyn.

They sneer: "The fellow does not even know
Which silver spoon to use for his dessert.
How could he know about big business then?
Suppose we talk of high finances or
Expense accounts, and there he goes and grabs
A knife, the wrong one too, to make a point.
That will not do. He's not the type we want
To hang around." They try to trip me up,
Because my tone's not couth enough for them
And I've the habit—somewhat masculine—
To call a spade a spade and not an instrument
For digging graves. They're prejudiced against me!
I can't rely but on the naked facts:
I'll scratch your back if you'll be scratching mine.
Madam, you're in the cauliflower trade
And so am I. That is the bridge between us.

    BETTY.

The bridge? How can you ever hope to bridge
The sea of blood you shed in Cicero?

    UI.

Experience has taught me it's no use
To try to reach you as a human being.
I'm talking to you, therefore, as a man
Of influence confronting you, the boss
Of one important export-import business.
And let me ask you bluntly: How is business?
That is the question, ma'm. Life marches on,
Regardless of death in the family.

    BETTY.

Yes, life goes on indeed and I will use it
To tell the world what pestilence you are.
You made this happy town your hell. Oh God,
I swear by Dullfeet's corpse that I will hate
My voice whene'er it says "Good morning!" or
"What's there for lunch?" instead of crying out
The one and only thing that must be cried:
Exterminate Ui!

GIRI. (*Menacingly.*)
                    Hey, baby, not so loud!
UI.
We're standing on God's little acre, ma'm.
I would expect a little more decorum.
Remember please: "How soon doth man decay!"
Or: "If you gotta go, you gotta go."
But business is immortal.
    BETTY.
                        Dullfeet! Oh,
I know now that you're gone from me!
    UI.
                                That's right.
Dullfeet is gone. Consider his departure.
Gone is the voice of Cicero to cry
Force! Terror! Violence! et cetera.
The loss is yours. Regret is not enough,
However deep. You stand without protection
In this here chilly world when weakness gets
Her teeth kicked in, which is a shame. The one
And only shield that's left for you is me.
    BETTY.
You say that to my face? I am the widow
Of the man you murdered. You monstrosity!
I knew you'd come because you always come,
Returning to the scene of crime, accusing
Others of your crime. "I didn't do it."
Or: "It was someone else!"—"I know from nothing!"
"Help, I've been raped!" cries Rape. And "Call the cops!
There's been a murder!" Mr. Murder cries.
    UI.
My mind's made up. Cicero needs protection.
And she shall have it soon, yes, any day.
    BETTY. (*Feebly.*)
Over my dead body.
    UI.
                    Whichever way.

BETTY.
Oh, God protect us from protectors!
UI.
                                        Well:
What is your answer, ma'm? Friendship forever?
(*Stretches out his hand.*)
BETTY.
Never! Never! Never! Never! Never!
(*Runs off, shuddering.*)

(*A sign appears: DOLLFUSS MURDER OPENS DOOR TO RAPE OF AUSTRIA. NAZIS WOO AUSTRIAN PUBLIC OPINION.*)

SCENE SEVENTEEN

Ui's bedroom at the Mammoth Hotel. Ui is having a nightmare, tossing and turning on his bed. His BODYGUARDS *sit dozing, guns in their laps.*

UI.
Hence, bloody shadows! Mercy! Go away!

(*The wall behind* UI *becomes transparent.* ERNESTO ROMA'S *ghost appears, a bullet hole in his forehead.*)

ROMA.
And all that will not help you. Not at all.
All murder, fraud and foaming at the mouth,
And be you spitting lickspittle or threat
It's all in vain, in vain. The roots are rotten.
Your crimes will never blosson forth, Arturo.
Treason is bad manure. Go lie and slaughter.
Cheat all the Clarks and murder all the Dullfeets!
But don't you touch your own men. Plot against the
   world,
But not against your fellow-plotters, please!

Tell barefaced lies to everybody's face
But not the face you're facing in the mirror.
You struck yourself down when you struck me down.
I was devoted to you in the days
When you were just a shadow falling down
The flophouse floor whose warmth we shared together.
And now I shiver in the draft of all
Eternity, while you go dining with
Your mighty friends. Treason has made you big.
Treason will make you fall. The way you did
Betray me, me your friend and aide, you will
Betray them all, And in the end, Arturo,
They'll all betray you one by one by one.
Green grass grows over Ernie Roma now,
Not over you and your disloyalty!
It's swinging in the breeze above the graves
Like someone hung up by his toes. It is
Observed by all, this faithlessness of yours,
Especially by those who dig your grave.
The day will come when everyone you smashed
Will rise. Arise, arise will all the men
Already crushed and to be crushed tomorrow.
And they'll be marching down the street to you,
A bloody world and full of hate. You'll stand
And look around for help. That's how I stood.
Then will you beg and bully, curse and lie.
No one will hear you. No one heard me cry.

    UI. (*Wakes affrighted.*)
Shoot! There! A traitor! Hence, you horror! The roof
Is falling.

(*He points at a spot on the wall. The* BODYGUARDS *start
    firing at it.*)

    ROMA. (*Fading away.*)
Shoot! What's left of me is bulletproof.

SCENE EIGHTEEN

Downtown Chicago. Mass-meeting of the Chicago GROCERS. *They are chalk-white in the face.*

FIRST GROCER.
Murder! Butchery! Blackmail! Robbery! Fraud!
    SECOND GROCER.
What's worse: Subservience and cowardice!
    THIRD GROCER.
Who is subservient? When January last
The first two mobsters walked into my store
And waved their guns, I gave them the old fisheye.
I calmly told them, "Gentlemen, I won't
Give in unless you make me," which they did.
I left no doubt I won't associate
With riffraff like the likes of them. What's more,
I made it clear I disapprove severely
Of their behavior. I was tough as nails.
I looked them in the eye to indicate:
"Okay, so here's the cash box, gentlemen.
I'd fight for it except you've got the guns."
    FOURTH GROCER.
Damn right you are. I wash my hands of it.
I said so to my wife.
    FIRST GROCER. (*Vehemently.*)
                        What cowardice?
It's common sense. Okay, I did shut up.
Grinding my teeth, I let them shake me down.
But I've had every reason to believe
These animals would stop their fireworks.
They didn't, Well, so there's this reign of terror
With murder, blackmail, fraud and robberies.
    SECOND GROCER.
Maybe there's something wrong with us. No backbone!
    FOURTH GROCER.
You mean no tommy guns. What can I do?
I'm not a gangster, I sell cauliflower.

THIRD GROCER.
Our only hope is this: Someone someday
Will stand up to the bastard. Let him try
This game some other place, and you will see . . .

(*Enter the* GROCERS *of Cicero. They are as white as
    chalk.*)

CICERO GROCERS.
Hello, Chicago!
  CHICAGO GROCERS.
                 Hello, Cicero.
What are you doing here?
  CICERO GROCERS.
                        We have been ordered
To be here.
  CHICAGO GROCERS.
          By whom?
  CICERO GROCERS.
                    By him.
  FIRST CHICAGO GROCER.
                          Ssh, not so loud.
  SECOND CHICAGO GROCER.
How can you let him tell you what to do?
Why do you let him order you about?
  THIRD CHICAGO GROCER.
Why don't you tell him go and fuck himself?
  FIRST CICERO GROCER.
He's got a gun, that's why, you genius!
  SECOND CICERO GROCER.
We're only giving in to force, you know.
  FIRST CHICAGO GROCER.
Goddam timidity! What are you, mice or men?
Are there no judges left in Cicero?
  FIRST CICERO GROCER.
None.
  THIRD CICERO GROCER.
    Not any more.

THIRD CHICAGO GROCER.
                    Listen, you must resist!
This plague of locusts must be stopped, you people!
The sky is black from them. They chew the flesh
From off our bones. They eat the country bare!
    FIRST CHICAGO GROCER.
First one town, then another. Who is next?
You've got to fight them to the bitter end.
    SECOND CICERO GROCER.
Why me?
    THIRD CICERO GROCER.
            Why me?
    FIRST CICERO GROCER.
                    No, thank you very much.
I wash my hands of it.
    FOURTH CHICAGO GROCER.
                    Our only hope was this:
Someone someday will stand up to the bastard.

(*FANFARE. Enter* ARTURO UI *and* BETTY DULLFEET
    [*in mourning*], *surrounded by* CLARK, GIRI, GIVOLA
    and BODYGUARDS.)

    GIRI.
Hello, you suckers. Everybody here
From Cicero?
    FIRST GROCER.
            Yes, sir.
    GIRI.
                    Chicago too?
    FIRST CHICAGO GROCER.
All here.
    GIRI. (*To* UI.)
            All hands on deck.
    GIVOLA.
                    My fellow grocers,
Welcome, thrice welcome. Hearty greetings from
The Cauliflower Trust. Dear Mr. Clark,
You're on.

CLARK.
                I've come to bring you news, my friends.
After negotiations lasting sev'ral weeks
—They haven't always been entirely smooth;
But hush! I mustn't gossip! Here's the score:
The Dullfeet Company has merged with us.
Which means that in the future you'll receive
Your vegetables from the Trust alone.
Your gain's too obvious for words. Increased
Security and prompt delivery,
New prices, slightly higher than before
But fixed already for the common good.
And here's the newest member of the Trust—
Dear Mrs. Dullfeet, let me shake your hand.

(CLARK *and* BETTY DULLFEET *shake hands.*)

GIVOLA.
Attention, all! Arturo Ui speaks!

(UI *mounts the rostrum.*)

UI.
Men of Chicago and of Cicero!
Friends, fellow citizens, and all without!
When aging Dogsborough, that honorable sage,
God bless his memory, appealed to me
One year ago, with tears in both his eyes:
"Protect Chicago's vegetable trade!"
I felt quite overwhelmed though skeptical
If I could justify his gratifying trust.
Now Dogsborough is dead. His testament
Is here for all the world to see. In words
As plain as applepie he calls me Son,
And thanks me, deeply moved, for all I've done
Since I obeyed that fatal day his summons.
The vegetable business, be it leeks.
Or lima beans, or heaven knows what else.

Is under firm protection in Chicago.
And this is due—false modesty be damned!—
To my determined handling of the game.
And when, quite unexpectedly, there came
Another man, Ignatius Dullfeet, too,
Offering the same proposal about Cicero,
I wasn't disinclined to place the town
Under my own protection likewise. But
I named at once my one condition, namely:
I will not do it 'less you want me to.
I must be asked by freely willed decision,
And thus I laid the law down to my men:
"Don't put the screws on Cicero, not yet!
The city must be fully free to choose!"
But I won't tolerate no hebetude,
No cranky Oke-doke, no sulky Very well!
Half-assed assent is no damn good to me.
Thus I demand, you men of Cicero,
A hearty, smarty, happy, snappy Yes!
And here! and now! and nothing less will do!
I want the works! And so I ask again:
Chicago men who know me from before,
And do appreciate me, I presume,
Who is for me? And let me incidentally add:
Whoever is not for me is against me,
And let him face the consequences. Now
You're free to vote.

   GIVOLA.

                 Before you vote, my friends,
Let's listen to our Mrs. Dullfeet first.
She's known to all, the widow of the man
Who's been so dear to one and all.

   BETTY.

                     My friends,
The man who was your friend, a friend to all,
Devoted husband, editor crusading,
Ignatius Dullfeet . . .

GIVOLA.

May he rest in peace!

BETTY.

Can't be your present help and pillar anymore.
I do advise you place your confidence
In Mr. Ui's hands as I have done.
I've had the chance to get to know him well
In these our dire days, a time so hard
For me to bear.

GIVOLA.

Let's vote.

GIRI.

Okay, you guys.
All those in favor of Arturo Ui,
Go stick 'em up! I mean, do raise your hands!

(*Some* GROCERS *immediately raise their hands.*)

A CICERO GROCER.
D'you mind if I go home?

GIVOLA.

But not at all.
Here everybody's free to do 's he pleases.

(*The* CICERO GROCER *leaves hesitantly. Two* BODY
GUARDS *follow him out. A shot is heard.*)

GIRI.
What's your decision, men?

(*All raise their hands, each man both hands.*)

GIVOLA. (*To* UI.)

The voting's done.
Profoundly touched and tremulous with joy,
The grocers of Chicago and of Cicero
Give thanks to you for your protection, Chief.

UI.
I do accept your gratitude with pride.

My friends, when I, the simple son of Brooklyn,
Obscure and outa work some fifteen years ago,
Obeyed the call of Providence, alone,
Except for seven buddies tried and true,
To wend my way to great Chicago town,
Determined to establish peace on earth,
Or I should say, the vegetable trade,
Ours was a little host but most fanatical
In our desire for peace. There's many of us now,
And no one laughs the way they used to laugh.
No one would dare to call me crank or hick,
That funny little man, the fringe lunatic,
And no more jeering, That's a lot of hooey,
That Arturo Ui. No more of that.
Peace in Chicago's vegetable marts
Is not a dream but grim reality
Which to assure against our enemies,
Today I ordered prompt delivery
Of Tommy guns and hand grenades, and naturally
Some brass knuckles and rubber truncheons too,
And new supplies of armored cars as well.
Because they're screaming for protection everywhere,
Not only in Chicago and in Cicero
But many other towns: Detroit!
Washington and Milkwaukee! Baltimore!
Toledo! Tulsa! Pittsburgh! Little Rock!
Wherever else they're selling groceries!
St. Louis! Boston! Minneapolis!
Yes, everybody wants protection now!
Flint! Scranton! Trenton! Charleston! Wilkes-Barre!
New York! New York today! The world tomorrow!

(DRUMS and FANFARE.)

*(A sign appears: MARCH 11, 1938: NAZI INVADE
    AUSTRIA. 98% OF TERRORIZED ELEC-
    TORATE VOTES YES FOR HITLER.)*

EPILOGUE

The actor who plays ARTURO UI *comes forward and takes
his moustache off to speak the epilogue.*

If we could learn to look instead of gawking,
We'd see the horror in the heart of farce,
If only we could act instead of talking,
We wouldn't always end up on our arse.
This was the thing that nearly had us mastered;
Don't yet rejoice in his defeat, you men!
Although the world stood up and stopped the bastard,
The bitch that bore him is in heat again.

THE END OF THE PLAY

OTHER TITLES AVAILABLE FROM SAMUEL FRENCH

THE RIVERS AND RAVINES
Heather McDonald

Drama / 9m, 5f / Unit Set
Originally produced to acclaim by Washington D.C.'s famed
Arena Stage. This is an engrossing political drama about the
contemporary farm crisis in America and its effect on rural
communities.

"A haunting and emotionally draining play. A community of
farmers and ranchers in a small Colorado town disintegrates
under the weight of failure and thwarted ambitions. Most of
the farmers, their spouses, children, clergyman, banker and
greasy spoon proprietress survive, but it is survival without
triumph. This is an *Our Town* for the 80's."
– *The Washington Post*

OTHER TITLES AVAILABLE FROM SAMUEL FRENCH

OUTRAGE
Itamar Moses

Drama / 8m, 2f / Unit Set

In Ancient Greece, Socrates is accused of corrupting the young with his practice of questioning commonly held beliefs. In Renaissance Italy, a simple miller named Menocchio runs afoul of the Inquisition when he develops his own theory of the cosmos. In Nazi Germany, the playwright Bertolt Brecht is persecuted for work that challenges authority. And in present day New England, a graduate student finds himself in the center of a power struggle over the future of the University. An irreverent epic that spans thousands of years, *Outrage* explores the power of martyrdom, the power of theatre, and how the revolutionary of one era become the tyrant of the next.

OTHER TITLES AVAILABLE FROM SAMUEL FRENCH

THREE YEARS FROM "THIRTY"
Mike O'Malley

Comic Drama / 4m, 3f / Unit set

This funny, poignant story of a group of 27-year-olds who have known each other since college sold out during its limited run at New York City's Sanford Meisner Theater. Jessica Titus, a frustrated actress living in Boston, has become distraught over local job opportunities and she is feeling trapped in her long standing relationship with her boyfriend Tom. She suddenly decides to pursue her dreams in New York City. Unbeknownst to her, Tom plans to propose on the evening she has chosen to leave him. The ensuing conflict ripples through their lives and the lives of their roommates and friends, leaving all of them to reconsider their careers, the paths of their souls and the questions, demands and definition of commitment.

CPSIA information can be obtained at www.ICGtesting.com

232657LV00003B/54/P